Additional Pamelia Barratt novels:

Blood: The Color of Cranberries

An Ostentation

Gray Dominion

Malheur

Die Birken

Intersecting Parallels

BY

Pamelia Barratt

Plowshare Media
LA JOLLA, CALIFORNIA

Library of Congress Control Number: 2020950252
Barratt, Pamelia
Intersecting Parallels

ISBN: 978-1-7341443-2-1   (trade paperback edition)

Cover photograph adapted from images by Patara, used under license
from Shutterstock.com

Published by:
Plowshare Media
P.O. Box 278
La Jolla, CA 92038

PUBLISHER'S NOTES

This is a work of fiction.
While, as in all fiction, the literary perceptions and insights are
based on experience, all names, characters, places, and incidents either
are the products of the author's imagination or are used fictitiously,
and any resemblance to actual persons, living or dead,
business establishments, events, or locales, is entirely coincidental.
Except as discussed on page 183, no reference to any real person is
intended, except for the obvious, recognizable, public figures.

For information about permission to
reproduce selections of this book, please write to:

Plowshare Media, P.O. Box 278, La Jolla, CA 92038
or visit PLOWSHAREMEDIA.COM

To the Stonehaven community

CONTENTS

MARCH, 1995

When Lena first moved to Quietwater, she couldn't believe her good fortune. Nestled into a canyon, her community was largely unknown to other San Diegans. Outsiders who risked driving through Quietwater hoping for a convenient shortcut would quickly find they were in a tangled maze of streets.

Twenty-five years ago, the developer had flooded the bottom of a canyon creating the two small lakes. He built two roads which ringed the lakes at different heights up the sloping canyon walls. To Lena's mathematical mind the lakes were like foci of concentric ellipses.

Each road in Quietwater held modest homes, all with lake views. At the canyon's top, the terrain flattened into what is known as a mesa. The developer built more homes on the mesa, but there, the roads were laid out in a grid pattern.

Lena lived in the mesa area, but her home was situated on the edge, overlooking the lower of the two lakes. Her actual house was similar to all the others. It had two levels. The garage faced the street. Some of the homes in Quietwater were attached, some were freestanding, some were rented, and some were owned. Hers was freestanding and rented.

This morning, like most, she got up early so she could walk before having to go to work. The ocean was less than a mile away. She could take her walk already dressed for work because at such an early hour the temperature was cool. The sun had not yet burned off the marine layer.

Today, she started on some mesa roads and then she would descend down to the lakes. Once at the bottom of the steep Coast Oak Drive, she would walk the footpath around the lower lake before returning to her home on Toyon Drive.

Toyon Drive: she smiled recalling how she had questioned the name of her street seven years ago when she first moved here from Moscow. Was it also of Spanish origin, like most other place-names in San Diego? A little research informed her that toyon was a type of tree. Soon thereafter, she recognized that all the streets in Quietwater had names of trees. That first year she made a point to identify each of the fifteen species so honored by the developer. She discovered, to her satisfaction, that there were four lemonade berry trees growing on Lemonade Berry Drive. But such consistency was not the norm. There was not a single ceanothus on Ceanothus Drive, and to her knowledge, there was only one ceanothus in all of Quietwater, and that was on Torrey Pine Drive! Such inconsistency bothered her.

Once Lena started walking on Palo Verde Drive, her spirits brightened. Although a short road, it led her to Jacaranda Drive— the loveliest street of all Quietwater. Positive thoughts started flowing through her mind, remembering how temperatures in Moscow in early March stayed firmly below freezing. How lucky she was to be living here.

She felt herself relaxing. Even though now the jacarandas showed no hint of their violet-shaded trumpet flowers, she knew they would come out in late May. Meanwhile, she was quite satisfied with the understory of Mexican sage. She had just read that it was the sepals of the Mexican sage that were purple, not the flower. Savvy hummingbirds only probed the white part for nectar.

She would find it hard to give up the diversity of San Diego's plants, not to mention hummingbirds, if she was called back to Russia. The thought of leaving this ideal climate (and all that came with it) to return to living in a cement-block apartment building with inadequate facilities was unbearable.

She and her two housemates had moved to San Diego seven years ago. By this time, they had each found their own niche. George had his beer buddies that he met at the Irish Pub. He had other friends too, like the ones with whom he went to baseball games. When they had finished their training in Moscow, Lena remembered George expressing his disappointment that football (soccer) was not popular in the United States. Once here, however, he had little difficulty transferring his sports enthusiasm to baseball. Lena marveled at his adaptability. He not only followed baseball religiously, he loved pizza, beer, and corny TV shows. His cotton candy grit helped to make him a pleasant housemate.

She could not say the same for Steve. Now in his mid-twenties, Steve was still as secretive and petulant as he had been as a teenager. A few years ago, she and George realized that Steve had become obsessed with a girl in the community. At first he talked about her incessantly, after seeing her jogging nearby. To avert trouble, George told Steve that a relationship with her was far too risky. "You can enjoy looking at her from a distance, but she shouldn't become aware of you. Any female that lives in Quietwater is out of bounds. Do you understand?"

He said he understood and he never mentioned her again, but Lena wasn't sure he could discipline himself. The man was a talented engineer. He cycled with a group of other young people on most weekends, and he often went rock climbing with a club he had joined. Of the three of them, Steve seemed the most American. He quickly picked up local mannerisms and expressions.

But Steve had a Jekyell-and-Hyde personality. Lena did not like his drinking. He had developed a taste for vodka in the old country. To give him credit, he seemed to know that Vodka was not as popular in America and restricted his practice to their home, and in particular, to his bedroom. Lena felt his drinking encouraged his quick temper and occasional outbursts of violence.

She recalled the night Steve almost killed Felice, George's young cat. George was out at a game, and Felice, who was probably in heat for the first time, started howling at 7:00 P.M. After a half hour, Steve grabbed the poker from the fireplace and went after her. Lena ran to open the front door so the cat could escape. Felice barely made it up the pear tree in time. The next morning, after Lena had left for work, George had to call his Quietwater chess buddy to help him get Felice down from the tree. Before day's end, George had taken Felice to the vet to be spayed.

When George and Steve resumed talking civilly to each other, Lena reminded them both that the incident came close to blowing their cover.

"You mean my cover," Steve corrected.

"No, our cover, once one of us is exposed, in time, we all will be." Did her lecturing do any good? She could only hope so.

Lena was now walking down the steep incline of Coast Oak Drive. She had to watch her step and couldn't let her thoughts distract her. Some parts of the sidewalk were uneven. As she approached Aleppo Pine Drive, the middle ellipse road, she changed her mind. She could walk the footpath around the lower lake another day. She wanted to check on a plant that she had successfully identified as Heavenly Bamboo only yesterday. Why that name? From what she could see, there was little resemblance to bamboo. It was in front of a house with a sign that said "Word for the Day."

Lena had stepped off the sidewalk to get closer to the plant. While bending over to inspect it, the front door opened and out came a woman in her bathrobe. Lena had to think fast. It would be rude just to walk away. The woman looked embarrassed, probably because she was outside in her bathrobe. Lena stood up straight and said: "I was just admiring your plant."

"Oh fine. Thank you. I only came out dressed like this to change the word for the day."

Lena then noticed she was carrying a narrow white board with a word written on it. To be polite, Lena asked what the word was for today.

"Today it's 'onomatopoeia,'" she answered, smiling while sliding the board into a stand in the front yard.

"Aha," Lena couldn't help herself, "like the bee is buzzing."

"Yes, exactly."

"The Coo-coo bird." Lena didn't wait for the woman's affirmation before adding: "The bacon is sizzling in the pan."

"The gurgling brook," the woman contributed laughing…. "Oh my, where do you live?"

Usually Lena would stop the conversation, but the woman's sweet smile made her change her mind. "I live on Toyon Drive. I have to take my walk early so I have enough time to get to work." That was as chatty as Lena could get. She started walking quickly down the sidewalk, then remembered her manners and turned around to look at the woman while saying: "Nice to talk with y… oh, ah…oh." Lena was on the ground. In trying to make a quick getaway, she had bumped into a metal junction box next to the sidewalk.

The woman quickly went to Lena. "Let me help you up. Are you all right?"

"Quite alright, thank you." Lena got up on her own as fast as she could and continued trying to walk naturally down the street.

"Let me at least drive you to your house," the woman called after her.

Lena was determined to keep on walking and didn't turn her head. "I'll be fine. Thanks for the word of the day."

Once home, Lena glanced at herself in the mirror. Some green blades needed to be brushed out of her dark wavy hair, but there were no grass stains on her slacks.

EMILY

Emily often had trouble falling asleep at night. She could be perfectly happy in daylight hours, but as soon as she was in bed with lights out, worries surfaced that she couldn't shrug off. Issues that became major after 11:00 P.M. were such things as what she had failed to get done that day, lamenting a hurtful remark she had made 5 years ago, many things to do with Ralph (Emily had lost her husband, Ralph, when she was 51), giving Holly Nields a D+ in chemistry. The list was endless.

During the day, she often had the opposite problem. Her fellow science teachers would bet on how many minutes into the teachers' meeting it would take for her to nod off. She finally caught on when she jerked awake and found them looking at her, glancing at the wall clock, and then smirking. She enjoyed the joke, but try as she would to pay attention, twenty minutes later drowsiness took over.

Tonight, her worrisome thoughts centered on Colton, her son. Where is he going with his life? She was certainly proud of him. Both she and Ralph had always been proud of him. As a child, he was unusually serious and focused. In his teenage years, he developed a consuming interest in Russia. He read many of the Russian classics in English. He studied the Russian language on his own and by taking Russian language classes at a local college while he was still in high school.

Now, Colton was 32 years old and an associate professor in Russian Studies at the University of California, San Diego. All that would be wonderful, if there was only something more. But there wasn't: not girls, not boys, not friends, nor sports. He's not even political, not a left-wing radical touting the advantages of communism. He was simply fascinated by all aspects of that large country: its diversity, its history, its literature, and its penchant for authoritarian regimes. It all interested him, but as Emily saw it, he had no agenda, no plan of how he would use his knowledge.

* * *

Emily and Colton had moved to San Diego in 1988. For about four years after the move, she ran an ongoing debate with herself in the wee hours: should she return to teaching high school chemistry? At first, she justified the delay because she had to get her new home functioning properly. Then she expanded the excuse to include needing to learn how to get around the city. But two years after the move, she still had not regained her enthusiasm for teaching. She debated between public school and private school. If she chose public, she would have to learn California history. That would be interesting, and good for her to know. A public school salary would be higher. On the other hand, Ralph's pension was perfectly adequate. She was never extravagant. Maybe she didn't need to earn money, at least not yet.

Public schools were co-ed and she wasn't used to teaching boys. Encouraging girls to follow a career in science had always been one of her primary goals. For centuries, women had been excluded from careers in science. Also, she liked teaching in a private school where she could design her own courses and labs. At Madeira, she had had the freedom to teach nuclear chemistry, which was not part of the core curriculum elsewhere. Emily was very aware she was living in a nuclear age. She had become an anti-nuclear activist ever since the Three Mile Island accident. Years later, she had been proud that her students could appreciate the seriousness of the Chernobyl tragedy.

By 1992, Emily had finally decided she would not continue teaching chemistry—period. Teaching had always consumed too much of her time and energy. She was starting to feel rebellious. Colton had just graduated from college at that point, and she felt they should celebrate that milestone by taking a trip together. There was no place he wanted to go to more than Russia. They left San Diego in early June to arrive in Moscow.

Moscow

Katya Drozdov graduated from Moscow State University's School of Journalism in 1980, but by that time, her education had hardly begun. Surprisingly, her place of birth had been New York City. Her parents were Soviet delegates to the UN. To be given such prestigious positions indicated that the Kremlin didn't fear that her parents would defect. Few communists were given permission to travel outside the Communist Bloc. In Soviet parlance, Katya was born with a soft red pillow under her head.

Upon graduation, she became a reporter for *Izvestia*, a newspaper that was the mouthpiece of the government. By 1983, she had married Sergei Drozdov, an officer in the navy. In anticipation of having a family, they rented a two-bedroom flat in one of Moscow's newer high-rises at Nizhegorodskaya 16.

After a year of marriage, Katya went to work for Aeroflot, the state owned airline. Up until this point, Katya had only experienced urban life in Moscow and St. Petersburg. Her exposure to rural areas was limited to vacationing at resorts. Her job with Aeroflot was to write articles for its magazine. As a top-level employee, she could fly anywhere in Russia at no personal expense.

She wrote articles to describe the variety of peoples in the federation, such as the Toflar Turkic-speaking people in Southern Siberia, who bred reindeer, or the red-haired Udmurt people of the central Urals. Such diversity became exciting to her, so she aimed to expose as many cultures of Russia's eleven different time zones as possible. She wanted her readers to appreciate the richness that came with the country's 185 ethnic groups.

Katya expected her career to continue in this vein, but Russia suddenly underwent a dramatic change—it had a new head of state: Mikhail Gorbachev. This new leader was a reformer. He began to decentralize the economy, and to tolerate criticism of the government. Gorbachev wanted to end the Cold War, which he felt was so devastating to the Russian economy.

In 1986, two huge explosions blew off the roof of one of the nuclear reactors at Chernobyl, 60 miles from Kiev. Four hundred times the radiation of the bomb dropped on Hiroshima was released. The accident occurred on April 26, but the world only became aware of it on April 28, when Swedish monitoring stations reported strong winds carrying a high amount of radioactivity. Katya and many others around the globe thought the soviet government tried to cover up the problem, and in so doing, put lives at stake.

Gorbachev said years later that it wasn't his perestroika or glasnost that brought down the Soviet Union, but Chernobyl. He resigned in 1991, and Boris Yeltsin became the first directly elected president in Russia's 1,000-year history. Yeltsin ended price controls, and began privatizing many of the assets of the former USSR.

By 1992, many Russians, including confirmed communists, were pleased their country was beginning to experience some of the freedoms felt in Western Europe. Reducing censorship opened up exciting possibilities. Pro-democracy newspapers began to start up. Katya switched jobs and became a columnist for the pro-democracy weekly, *Obshchaya Gazeta*.

In early June, Katya heard about and saw posters advertizing an anti-nuclear protest in Nimsky Square. It was to take place on Saturday. She wondered why Nimsky Square? It wasn't well known; it didn't front a government building which had anything to do with nuclear power. It probably wouldn't amount to much, but she thought she should check it out, as it could be a good topic for her column in the newspaper. Also, Nimsky Square wasn't far from where she lived. Sergei wanted to stay home and read. He needs time to himself she rationalized, and besides, sailors were forbidden to take part in political demonstrations.

Katya walked to the square. Perhaps the demonstrators had chosen a good location after all. There was a lot of foot traffic, two outdoor cafes, and some other shops. She saw a crowd of about 200 protestors ahead. Some held signs. The day was chilly now, yet would probably warm up. There was a threat of rain, but judging from the sky, Katya only expected a drizzle, not a downpour. As she approached, she thought that a couple hundred people was actually a good turnout—a decent number, considering that Russia had only started tolerating demonstrations two years ago.

The crowd was composed of many ages. In fact, looking around, Katya realized that some of the participants were foreign. She overheard one speaking German. She saw a man wearing a beret. Awhile later, she heard a man shouting out comments in pretty good Russian, with a slight American accent. She finally spotted the source of that voice. He was tall and wearing jeans and a plaid shirt.

Seeing his jeans diverted her thoughts. For decades, people in the Eastern Bloc wanted to wear jeans. About five years ago, Russia had started producing an inferior version that wasn't as popular. Recently, she had heard that Muscovites could legally buy Levis, actual Levis. She smiled to think that the "jean crime" days were over.

Katya kept watching the American. Occasionally, he would bend down and say something to an older woman standing next to him. She noticed a resemblance. The same thick eyebrows and pointed nose. The woman might be his mother. Katya edged closer to hear them talk. Yes, they are Americans. It took her a moment to realize the significance. They're Americans, she repeated to herself. To think we're getting American tourists now, and they're allowed to participate in an anti-government protest! Phenomenal! Would she dare to bring them into the story she would write? How did they find out about the protest? She laughed at herself. Her hopes were getting away from her.

They were probably just walking by.

She noticed that she wasn't the only one watching them. It was exhilarating to be with a former enemy and promoting together a common goal. Katya couldn't help herself. She had to ask them where they were from.

"San Diego, California."

"Really, so far away!" She wasn't sure where in California San Diego was, but she knew California was far away on the western coast. "Welcome to Russia." Others were listening. Katya didn't know if she should speak in Russian or English, but her English was poor so she chose Russian. "What brings you to our country?"

The man translated Katya's question for the woman, who then smiled and said: "You...this protest is a major reason we came." The man continued to translate. Katya was surprised that the woman had a lot to say. "...ever since the accident at Three Mile Island...."

Katya responded, using Colton as the go-between: "Many of us Russians were dubious about the safety of our reactors, and we knew we couldn't trust anything the government told us." Katya's pride took over: "Although we are few in numbers here at this demonstration, in the last two years, our protests have stopped a new nuclear reactor from being constructed."

Conversing was difficult with demonstrators shouting around them. Katya hoped they hadn't noticed her eyes tearing up.

The young man was called Colt, she learned, and he had just graduated from university in Russian Studies, no less. The woman, Emily, was his mother, just as Katya had suspected. Evidently, between mother and son, mother was the major protestor. But how grand it was to speak to her son, who was almost fluent in Russian!

Toyon Household

Moving into the house on Toyon in 1988 was their first immersion into life in the United States for all three of them. Although they knew the Soviets were prepared to finance their sleeper cell until it was self-supporting, Lena began looking for a job right away, and landed one that was relatively high-paying and in the field of her PhD—computer science. Steve and George didn't find jobs until a year later.

Whereas both George and Steve soon found things to do outside the home (and people to do them with), Lena was at a loss to know what to do, especially on the weekends. She had wanted to blame her inability to make friends on the fact that she was always working, but she knew she had had the same problem when living in Moscow. She didn't think it was her lack of friends that bothered her. It was not having more things to do, besides reading books and taking walks. The books had to be in English (Soviet rules) and had be on the topics that Americans liked to read (Soviet suggestions).

Her room was soon overflowing with books. She was delighted when she learned from her handler about the Little Library on Scott Street. Getting to it involved walking several blocks away from the Quietwater community. His reason for telling her about the Little Library had nothing to do with her excess of books, but she saw no reason why she couldn't use it to deposit books she no longer wanted. She never put her name in them, nor did she underline passages, or write notes in their margins.

In Moscow, being a fly on the wall was to her advantage. It had kept her safe. She was never seen as a threat. In the United

States, as a spy, it was an advantage as well. She didn't have to force herself to keep a low profile. It came naturally to her.

The household soon developed a routine that allowed them to operate efficiently. Lena bought the groceries and cooked the meals. That made sense because she was posing as the wife and mother—the much younger wife of George and the almost-too-young mother of Steve. Nobody ever questioned her role in the family because she remained unexposed to other people.

This said, Lena hadn't considered going to the public library right away. Once in the downtown Central Library, she found she could read newspapers and magazines from all over the world, without anyone knowing it. She was thrilled to catch up on Russian politics. Evidently, from what she read, Russia was in chaos. Gorbachev had introduced some reforms that she had thought would never come about. It was now permissible to criticize the government and its policies. That was also what she thought she had heard on her car radio.

What she didn't comprehend was that when Yeltsin became president, he tried to introduce even more reforms than Gorbachev had; reforms such as private ownership. This she found difficult to believe. Furthermore, Yeltsin abolished the Soviet Union. Just amazing! Could all this be true? If so, it would be a cause for celebration. But a darker thought came to her: Will this new Russia want to continue having sleeper cells in the United States? Lena directed all her cognitive skills to answer this question—the $64,000 question (even questions have price tags in the States!). She, George, and Steve were illegals, the name the Soviets gave to sleeper agents. Are illegals no longer relevant?

If her time in San Diego was limited, she shouldn't waste it. It could be coming to an end. She told herself to spend more time enjoying life while she still could; making friends, going out, doing things, traveling. She knew she wouldn't follow through on this logic, but if nothing else, she was uplifted and felt a new freedom.

GREG

Still lying in bed with the covers pulled up to his chin, Greg looked through his window, making sure not to check the time on the wall clock. He saw that there was a heavy mist filling the canyon over the lake. That means the sun is thirty or forty minutes from rising above the eastern hills, he figured. Hmm, it's about 7:10 A.M. Only then did he check the clock on the wall: 7:20 A.M. Not bad. He was getting better.

Now he had to get up. Oh, the joys of being retired! In his mind it was perfectly acceptable to rise between 6:45 and 7:45. Earlier than 6:45 meant he was obsessive about something. Later than 7:45 probably meant he was lazy, although that was still up for debate.

He threw on a pair of shorts and a smelly T-shirt and went for his morning jog around the two lakes. He knew he was jogging slower these days. Ten years ago, he could have made it around both lakes in twelve minutes. Now, it was getting closer to twenty.

Greg liked to go early because it gave him a chance to check the condition of the path and determine if there had been any nefarious activities going on the previous night. The pathway was not lit at night, and all the homes at this bottom level of the canyon were set back from it, shielded by dense bushes. "Outsiders" and perhaps, some "insiders" could be up to no good.

At board meetings, he chuckled to himself when he heard these complaints. The first suspected of doing no good were homeless people. They were outsiders of the lowest order. Claims that there were encampments in the woods near the lakes were frequently made. Actual evidence was rarely retrieved. The second to be accused were outsiders using dope; higher up the list were office workers who had the nerve to want to stroll around the lakes on their luncheon breaks. Some outsiders drove into Quietwater and parked near the lakes, bringing children with them, or worse still, their dog. "It's our property," was a frequent claim. About once a year, the pitch rose to suggest that all of Quietwater be gated.

His years of service on San Diego's police force put Greg in high demand with some insiders to be on the HOA board. When he retired, he no longer had an excuse. Oh well, it gave him something to do. With Trina having passed and their two kids moved to the East Coast, he had more time on his hands than he wished for. Reading, code puzzles, gardening, and making repairs were all enjoyable, but couldn't compare with close personal relationships.

Oops, there's a needle. Greg used a leaf to pick it up then went to the doggie bag dispenser. Once in a bag, he still had to be careful. The needle could easily poke through it. He made a point of remembering the place where he found it so he could tell the board. There was a small pull-off from Laurel Sumac Drive, big enough for three cars to park by the lower lake, in a fair bit of seclusion. Greg believed that this location was where many nighttime shenanigans started. Perhaps, a motion sensitive light would help with security.

At the next board meeting, numerous issues were brought forward during the public comment time. The most frequent complaints involved cars and dogs. The towing fee could be as high as $300: "But my car was simply parked in front of my own house."

One woman claimed her dog was on a leash. "The CC&Rs never said I had to hold on to the other end." The community seemed divided about dogs. Some felt every dog should always be on a leash, no matter how well behaved it was. Others took pride in showing off how obedient their Charlie, Alfie, or Otis was when off leash. It was true that the only thing that could be pinned on Beaufort was his drooling.

Serving on the board, like policing, exposed Greg to a wide range of characters and featherweight crimes. Occasionally, emotions ran high. Board members were like teachers breaking up a fight on the school playground. Some poor soul received a poison pen letter because his car blocked access to the sidewalk. There was one woman who was an astronomy enthusiast who stayed up much of the night to see the stars. She slept until 10:00 in the morning. A year ago, she claimed a large object flew over the lakes one night. Ever since, the board members called her 'UFO' among themselves. Another woman, named Morgan, attended every board meeting for years and kept meticulous records of BOD decisions and never hesitated to point out the board's contradictions, omissions, or failure to follow the CC&Rs.

There were advantages to being on the board. It gave Greg an opening to speak to people he was interested in. He discovered George Hansen loved to play chess. Now, they got together for a game at the community center twice a month. George was a happy-go-lucky guy, but was dead serious when playing chess.

Being on the board helped Greg get to know Emily Dunn, a widow who had moved here from Washington, D.C. She kept asking Greg for advice. "How should I go about getting the steps down to the backyard fixed?" Her son Colton was some high-brow intellectual who didn't know a flat head from a Phillips. Emily always needed help with something or other. At first, he thought she was just using him as a free handyman. Her deceased, Ralph, wrote for *National Geographic*, which certainly put the man in a different class than Greg.

Emily told him stories about when she taught chemistry and planetary science at a private girl's boarding school in McLean, VA. "My students were daughters of diplomats who had overseas assignments." Did she think he would be impressed?

He shared with her some of his experiences patrolling the City Heights area of San Diego, breaking into a drug-fest and barely getting out with his life. He laid it on extra thick, just to shut her up about that school, Madeira. They couldn't have named it McLean School for Girls. No, it had to be Madeira.

In Emily's spare time, she had been an anti-nuclear activist. To draw her out, Greg asked: "What sign did you carry?"

She looked out over the canyon in a nostalgic gaze: "'Mothers against Nuclear Power.' I almost brought my sign with me when we moved here."

Greg could remember seeing anti-nuclear protestors on TV in the '80s. It seemed to him that recently, the attitudes of all types of protestors were hardening. "You probably view the police as German Shepherds nipping at your heels." She perked up and was about to answer, but before she took off, he wanted to set her straight. "Yeah, what we wear may be uniform, but not our opinions." She remained quiet, so he went on: "For sure, it was stupid to build the San Onofre Nuclear Reactor on an earthquake fault line. You know, the power plant up the coast at San Clemente? Using the ocean for cooling purposes may have been cheap, but the marine life is now in jeopardy. That was stupid, too."

Over the next year they added to this discussion, sometimes while enjoying a glass of wine on her deck. When they first started seeing each other, she was always immaculately dressed, wearing jewelry and makeup. Lately, he noticed some sloppiness—shirttails out, flip flops, and baggy trousers. She seemed happier and he felt more comfortable with her. She's adjusting to California, he thought.

CHECHNYA

With books to read, Lena didn't mind shutting herself in her room after work. There were still times when Steve's drinking made her nervous. She also disliked hearing the insipid TV shows George loved to watch. She was only sociable with her housemates while she cooked the evening meal or while they ate dinner together at the table. Books had always been her refuge.

Since discovering the Central Library several years ago, it occurred to her that she could research topics with anonymity here in San Diego, a luxury she never enjoyed in Moscow. The topic that most interested her was Chechnya, where she spent her early childhood. She never trusted what she heard or read about Chechnya while she lived in Russia.

Chechnya is a region in the Caucasus Mountains between the Caspian and Black Seas. From what Lena read, it had been a contentious area going back to the time of Catherine the Great. The tsarina wanted to annex Chechnya so Russia would have a bridgehead against the Ottoman Empire and Iran, as well as to extend Russia's Black Sea coastline. Assimilating Chechens into her empire was not easy, even back then. Slavic Orthodox Russians were never comfortable accepting the culture, language, and Islamic religion of the mountainous Chechen people. The feeling was mutual.

Lena was born in Grozny, the capital of Chechnya. Her name was originally Lena Vakhaev. From what she could remember, her family was poor. Without brothers or sisters, she spent her time, as she recalled, playing outside with other children, even in the cold winters. When she was eight years old, her parents disappeared. People suspected that they had either been killed or kidnapped. She never saw them again. She was temporarily sheltered by another family in Grozny, the Okueva family. They had known her parents, and from them, she learned that her grandparents on her father's side had also disappeared many years ago. Lena didn't remember them at all.

Through her research at San Diego's Central Library, Lena was able to piece together some of her family's sketchy history. Evidently, Stalin forcibly relocated around 500,000 people from the Chechen region in 1944. They were sent to the frozen steppes of northern Kazakhstan to work in forced labor camps. 'Uncle Joe's' excuse was that Chechens had colluded with the Nazis during the Second World War. As far as Lena could determine, his claim had never been substantiated. Stalin encouraged ethnic Russians to move into Chechnya. Thirty percent of the dislocated Chechens perished in Kazakhstan, before Khrushchev repatriated the survivors in 1956.

If her grandparents had returned to Grozny in 1956, Lena surmised, she would have been three years old. Surely they would have reconnected with her parents, but Lena had no memory of them, so she deduced that they must not have survived the labor camp.

Igor Yurin, a Russian soldier stationed in Grozny, must have made some arrangement with the Okueva family, because when Lena was about ten, she started living in Moscow with the Yurin family. That was when Lena's name changed to Lena Yurin.

When she first went to Moscow to live with the Yurin family, she was grateful just to have food, shelter, and a chance to go to school. She didn't mind that they looked to her to be their servant. By the time she was 13, she realized they were interested in her. They started giving her as much food as their other children. When friends popped in, Lena was the first of the children to be introduced. The Yurins asked her questions that would show off her knowledge to their guests. Lena did not like being singled out, but similar changes occurred in school. She finished high school two years ahead of her age group. From then on, her education was taken out of her family's hands. She was swooped up by the Directorate S, a mysterious agency within the SVR (Sluzhba Vneshney Razvedki), which was Russia's Foreign Intelligence Service. Under this agency, Lena was led and trained to be a sleeper agent. Her name was changed to Lena Hansen. She finally met her 'husband' George Hansen and her 'son' Steve Hansen when she arrived in San Diego.

* * *

By 1995, Lena was satisfied with what she had learned about her roots in Chetnya and started concentrating on other aspects of Russia: its politics and culture. Her walks around the lakes had opened her to new topics of study: trees and plants, both identification and characteristics. Now, she was learning about birds, trying to distinguish between those that were in San Diego year-round, those that were spring visitors, those that just migrated through, and those that were winter visitors.

As intellectually fulfilling as these interests were, they couldn't compensate for her loneliness. Lena wanted a friend. One day, on her long morning walk, she became aware that many people walking the lakes were enjoying the companionship of a dog. Lena started thinking that a dog of her own might be the solution. Caring for another creature, especially one that gave unconditional love, was what she needed.

But if she had a dog, she would have to keep him in her bedroom. Steve was capable of outbursts of cruelty. He couldn't be trusted with any animal in the house. Maybe she could take the dog to work with her? Would that be allowed?

Her office at General Atomics was small but conveniently located adjacent to that of her boss, Art Campbell. Her job was to debug coding applications for GA's drone construction. This meant she had to clean up whatever sections of code that she was given to work on. She had to remove glitches and make the programming flow better. At any one time, she was never given the drone's entire code, known as 'the package.' It was probably on the computers of only a few of the company's top engineers, of whom Art was one. No one thought for a moment that she was clever enough to break into Art's computer. Lena was given a password that only opened the section of the package she was being asked to clean up. When she was finished, that password was changed.

She asked Art if she could bring a dog to work.

"Is the dog a barker?" Art asked.

"I haven't got it yet, but I will ask at the pound."

"A mutt, huh. They are always the easiest to train." Art digressed into describing various dogs he had owned over the years. Finally, he realized he was wasting time and someone else was waiting to see him outside his office door. "You can't let him roam around, you know."

"Yes, of course."

"How big is he?"

"About 13 pounds, if I can get the one I want."

"Well, we can try it," he said. "What will you name it?"

"Laika."

* * *

Lena had successfully retrieved the package from Art's computer a few times in the past. She just took her flash drive home with her in her purse. Later she would make it available to her handler through a dead drop.

Lena still had no idea who her handler was. She thought he was a man, but she never heard his voice. He could be a woman, for all she knew. If he needed to talk with her, he would text her using a burner phone. These procedures ensured that the caller could not be traced. Calls did not show up on the landline's phone bill for the Hansen residence.

Board Meeting

Greg got a phone call from Emily that morning. "I heard we're expecting a lot of rain."

"Let's hope so," he commented. "There have been fires in the East County for two weeks now. They're still not contained." The fires that summer were worse than the last. People worried about the Santa Ana winds from Arizona. They brought hot, dry weather conditions to San Diego at the time when the county's vegetation was in desperate need of water.

"The winds themselves don't start the fires," Emily said, "but they can keep them going for weeks."

"With devastating results," he added. Greg knew many of the fires were started by careless people and arson in the back country, but increasingly, the blame was falling on the poorly maintained grid system of their power company. All of this had been on Greg's mind when Emily called.

"They said we can expect possible thunderstorms."

"That would be good." Greg said, but he thought—she wants me to fix something. What's it going to be? Ah, something to do with rain, no doubt.

"You know the last time we had a lot of rain, my gutters overflowed. Should I have them cleaned?"

"Yes."

"I mean the water just gushed straight down at the corners of the house."

"Um-hm."

"That's bad for the foundation, isn't it?"

"Yes."

"Thank you so much for helping me fix those cracks in my foundation. When was that, a year ago?"

"Emily, I want two glasses of wine, red, and a delicious dinner. What was it you fixed for me last time?"

"Beef Bourguignon."

"I want that with roasted potatoes. I hope my ladder is long enough. And dessert, what can you make me for dessert?"

An hour later, Greg was up the ladder when he remembered that tonight was a board meeting at 7:00. He didn't want to rush Emily's dinner. So he asked her to have it the following night, instead.

"That's better. By then, the rain should be over and we can eat out on the deck."

"Fine, how's about throwing in an astronomy lesson?"

"I was just thinking the same thing." She held on tightly to the ladder. "Of course it may be cloudy."

"OK, we could have the astronomy lesson another night."

"Sounds good! Let's see, Colton arrives home from Russia tomorrow. I think his plane gets in at 4:00 in the afternoon."

"Damn!" Greg said under his breath.

"I imagine he'll be jet-lagged."

"I'll tuck him in," Greg said just loud enough so Emily heard him. Her smile was gratifying.

* * *

Greg rushed out of his home on Sycamore Drive, up on the mesa. The heavy rainfall had just stopped. The air was a pleasure to breathe in, clean and moist, a welcomed change from the recent hot dry weather. He looked up to find the moon. It was just coming out from behind a cloud. It's in the waning, no, in the gibbous phase, he decided. It's waxing. He hoped he had that right because he intended to impress Emily with his cleverness when he next saw her. For now, it was doing a good job at lighting his way to the community center.

The board meetings were always held in the community room. It was not an impressive room, rectangular in shape and with no windows. He was the last board member to arrive. He took his place at the long table facing the HOA members who came to the meeting. There were white stacking chairs for them to sit in. The floor was cement, so every time a chair moved, there was a grating sound.

The meeting started with the usual public comment session. Any homeowner was allowed to speak on an issue that concerned him or her for 3 minutes.

Ebony, who some privately called UFO, was the first to speak. "I saw it again last night." Looks were exchanged. A few smirked.

"And what time was that?" Board President Marco Romero, politely asked.

"Between 2 and 3 in the morning."

"When was the last time you saw it?"

Ebony couldn't remember exactly, but Morgan rapidly flipped back through the pages in her notebook. "Here it is. Six months ago. You reported it at the February 11th board meeting."

"Due to the sporadic timing, this will be difficult to track. Thank you for your vigilance," Marco said to Ebony. "Please continue to inform us. Who would like to speak next?"

Lawrence White, a man in his early 50s, rose. "I just wanted to ask about that house on the upper lake with the blinds all drawn. I live nearby. The whole time I've lived in Quietwater that house has been unoccupied. Is it in foreclosure? What's going on there?"

"No," Marco answered. "it appears that the owner just wants to hold onto the property. He…," Marco turned to another board member for clarification.

"The owner is a realty firm: 'Friendly Haven Realty.'"

"The firm pays the homeowners fees on time and maintains the grounds, so there is nothing we can do about it."

Lawrence held out his hands while raising his shoulders: "All that money and they don't even bother to rent it out." Lawrence sat down.

Next a chorus of three homeowners complained about dogs

off of their leashes. "Well, what's the board going to do about it?" one of them demanded.

"The first time they get a warning, the second, a fine of $50."

"Oooh, too high," others in the room said.

"Yes, Frank, did you want to say something?"

A frail old man stood. "I'm Frank. I live on Toyon Drive in unit 183. My next-door neighbor is continually making a loud grinding noise on weekends. It goes on all day. It is very unpleasant. Susannah, my wife, has Parkinson's disease and needs to rest during the day. It makes her upset."

"We'll look into it, Frank. You and Susannah were among the first residents of Quietwater. Is that right?"

"Yes, well, we were the third family who moved in."

"The grinding sounds like work that belongs in a factory, not a home. Have you spoken to your neighbor about it?"

"I tried to. They are the Hansens. I spoke to the son. I don't know his first name but the man was not very friendly. He just glared at me, so I went back home."

"Let's see, you're in unit 183, so which neighbor is it: unit 181 or 185?" There was confusion as board members tried to consult a map of Quietwater.

Morgan spoke up: "That's unit 185. The address is 2961 Toyon Drive."

"Thank you Morgan."

Greg knew what was coming.

"Greg, would you look into this?"

Walking home that night after the board meeting, it started to rain again. Greg should have worn his raincoat. He was startled to hear a clap of thunder seemingly nearby. Any thunder at all was rare for San Diego. Once home, he called Emily so see if her gutters were draining properly. He could have waited until morning, but he wanted to hear her voice.

"Oh yes, they've been draining perfectly. Thank you so much. How was the board meeting?'

"Yeah, a few funny stories to tell you!"

"Really? Should I hear them now? You could tell me over a glass of wine."

"Why not? I'll be there shortly." He chuckled when he realized wine was always their excuse to get together. It was her last night without Colton.

* * *

"Yes, that was my third trip to Russia."

Emily was working on dinner in the kitchen, giving Greg an opportunity to ask Colton some questions, before the conversation turned to Russian politics, literature, or history. Greg could be interested in those topics, but once Colton got started, it became more of a monologue than a conversation. "So you have always stayed at Katya and Sergei's house?"

"Not house—in Moscow almost everybody lives in apartments. Yes, I stay with them. They have an extra bedroom."

Greg had to suppress his urge to laugh. Colton would be the last person he'd ever suspect of hanky panky with any gender. Thank God his mother is not like him.

"Sergei is away a lot, you know, being in the Navy. Katya herself is actually gone from home much of the time. She covered the war in Chechnya, you know." (Greg didn't know.) "That was an incredible feat…."

When Colton took a breath, Greg quickly asked: "Where exactly is Chechnya?"

For another fifteen minutes, Colton filled Greg with the details that answered his question and more, but in that time, he realized that Colton was incapable of seeing what was around him. If Greg had slipped in that he was sleeping with his mother, Colton would just continue his monologue.

Emily came out to announce that dinner was ready. She looked terrific. Her blue blouse accentuated her eyes. The dinner was scrumptious. Colton started yawning during the entrée. Greg caught Emily's eye and winked. Before the last course, Colton excused himself. He was too tired for dessert, but turned to Greg and said: "Maybe you'd like to come to the lecture I'm giving at

UCSD. It's about the war in Chechnya and Yeltsin."

"When is it?"

"In a couple of weeks, on a Saturday night [yawn] at 7:00."

"I'd love to."

Colton turned to his mother. "Mom, a great dinner! I should go away more often. You must have been practicing cooking while I was gone [yawn]. Thanks, good night."

* * *

The next Saturday morning, Greg woke up early. He went through his usual routine: jog, shower, breakfast. He read and did a code puzzle before walking to George's house. By this time, 10:30 A.M., the grinding should have started. It was going to be a hot day, he thought. When he got to Toyon Drive, he was already perspiring. 2950, 2953, 2955…my God, he could hear the grinding noise from this distance—three houses away. It was high pitched and loud, like a dentist's drill. The noise was coming from the garage, definitely. It must be hotter than blazes inside there, but the door's kept shut. Why—thoughtfulness to the neighbors, perhaps?

After knocking several times, he realized that whoever was in there couldn't hear him, so Greg waited for an interval when the grinding stopped to pound on the front door again, suppressing his urge to say: "Police, open up." Thank God those days were over.

The door opened, a six-foot-tall young man in a gray undershirt and cutoff trousers looked down at Greg. "Yes?"

"Hello, I'm Greg McDonald." He smiled, but the man made no response. "I play chess occasionally with your father, George." As he spoke, Greg kept examining the young man's face for similar features to those of George. He saw none. Greg waited for a response.

Finally, the man said: "What do you want? Dad's not here."

"Well actually, it is you I want to speak to."

"I'm very busy right now."

"That is what I've come to talk to you about."

"Oh really?" A sour look came on his face, but he didn't respond further.

"The HOA board has received a complaint about the noise you are generating."

"The old man next door, is he the one who complained?"

"Yes, Frank Offenbacher is his name. What is your name?"

"If you're on the board you probably know my name. I'm Steve Hansen, George and Lena's son. Now look here, I have a project that is due in a week. I have to get it finished. I don't make noise after 5:00 P.M."

"Why didn't you explain that to Frank when he came to talk to you about the noise?"

"Look, where is this going? I've got to get back to my work."

"Frank and his wife, Susannah, deserve respect. They have lived peacefully in this community since it started and have never made a complaint. Susannah is ill and needs to be able to rest during the day."

"I'm not stopping her."

"What are you doing in your garage that makes so much noise?"

"None of your business! Now, I have to get back to work. It'll be over in a week." Steve turned around to go inside and shut the front door in Greg's face.

Greg was furious and wished he still had his badge, not that a badge would keep Steve from being rude. Being rude is a first amendment right. Nonetheless, Steve's lack of manners made him mad.

Walking back home gave him time to calm down and think. He would speak to George. The day they were due to play chess was coming up soon. In the meantime, he would suggest the board send Steve Hansen a warning notice. If the noise didn't stop within a week, a fifty dollar fine would be imposed. Greg stewed over this most of the afternoon.

Noisy Neighbor

Greg planned to drive by the Hansen's twice a day to check on the noise. After a couple of days he decided it would be better to have another witness. The other board members were quite busy with HOA chores. Who had more time than they knew what to do with? Somebody who's methodical and punctilious—of course, Morgan was the one to ask.

Greg's phone rang three days later. It was Morgan. "You've got to see what they're doing. It appears that they're putting in air conditioning and insulation. They have the garage door open, but you can only see in around the edges. I mean it's hard to explain, but there is a huge tarpaulin covering up the middle of the garage."

"Hmm. I guess the air conditioner should have been approved first, but adding insulation shows a positive response." Greg could understand installing air, if they had to keep the garage door shut, but why was that necessary? Is Steve making something illegal? Or is he running a business from his home, which the HOA doesn't allow?

Morgan also mentioned seeing a truck from a company that upgraded electricity. Greg figured an electrical upgrade could be required, if Steve was using heavy duty power tools. Maybe he's doing some soldering. What was the man working on, he wondered? He would certainly ask George about all this.

* * *

Greg waited to see if George would bring up the topic first. After seven moves on the chessboard, George said: "Hey, what's up with you, Gregory? Do you have something on your mind?

You shouldn't have moved your knight back then."

"Yes, I realize that now. Did Steve tell you that I went over to your house three days ago?"

"Really? No, he didn't."

Greg was flabbergasted that George didn't know. As Greg informed him of the purpose of his visit, George looked surprised and occasionally muttered things like: "Oh my God," or, "I had no idea."

Eventually, George said: "Look Greg, you have a son don't you? I think you said you did. Maybe as a policeman, you were able to discipline your son better. Our boy doesn't want to live with us, but he's an artist and makes little money. He begged us to let him have the garage for his studio. We promised him we would not go inside. These kids are awfully temperamental these days, don't you think?"

Greg said nothing, but just kept looking at George.

"Well, at least ours is. I think he makes mobiles, but Lena and I don't really know what he does in there. He did say a neighbor complained about the noise. That's why we're paying for the insulation and air conditioning."

"What about the upgrade of electricity?" Greg asked.

"Oh, the house has needed that for a long time. We thought we'd do it all at once."

"I see. Well, let's hope this will greatly reduce the noise level."

Did he ever tell George that he had been a policeman, or that he had a son? Maybe he had. Greg talked to so many homeowners. If Steve does make mobiles, what does he do with them? He needs money, so he must sell them. Greg would report all this to the board, but first, he wanted to see if those installations had reduced the grinding noise.

The following Saturday, Greg walked over to the Hansen home again. When he was in front of their house, only then could he hear a grating sound. The noise was significantly muffled. He thought he'd better check it out with Frank, next door.

"Yes, Greg, we hardly hear anything now. Thank you for

taking care of it. Susannah is very happy. She can rest on the weekends now."

Greg was feeling pleased with himself. It is rare to have homeowners respond so quickly after a complaint is filed against them. Their solution was extremely costly. Wait a minute, he said to himself, the Hansens are not *homeowners*, they're *renters*! In the afternoon, Greg looked in the HOA records to check. Yes, the actual owner was the Friendly Haven Real Estate firm in San Francisco, the same company who owned the vacant house on the upper lake. How could the Hansens get the firm's approval so quickly, especially when the improvement was so costly? Maybe the Hansens paid for it themselves. They have two wage earners. Maybe they could afford it, but they will never get that money back. It's unusual, no matter how you figure it. Oh well, that's not my concern. Everybody seems happy with the outcome.

* * *

Greg picked up Emily so they could go together to hear Colton's lecture at UCSD. Colton had warned them to allow plenty of time as there could be a long walk from where they would have to park to the Stevenson Auditorium. They had hoped to sit in the center section near the stage, but the hall had already been filling up, so they were forced to sit farther back than they would have liked.

"Colton will be pleased so many people are here. He's worked hard on this."

Greg wished Colton well. "This would be quite an achievement at any age, but especially for someone so young as Colton." Greg did a quick calculation of Colton's age: 34! Thirty-four and he's still living at home! Nonetheless, he was impressed with the young man's intellect. Greg himself had graduated from San Diego State University, a good university, but not of the same caliber as UCSD. Greg also knew that his particular major—Criminal Justice—did not cut it in intellectual circles.

When he first met Emily, he was intimidated by the credentials of her deceased husband Ralph: Yale, Johns Hopkins, and then working for the National Geographic Society as a writer. About two years into their friendship, Greg realized that Emily herself felt intimidated by Ralph's credentials. Although she had graduated from an Ivy League College, she told Greg she wasn't as bright as the typical Smithy. She had to work all the time to get her grades of Cs and Bs. Emily knew she was an over-achiever. She said that both Ralph and Colton had told her for years to 'lighten up.'

One of the many things that Greg loved about Emily was her honesty about herself. Once, when they were discussing Colton, she told Greg that Colton had inherited her obsessive behavior and Ralph's intelligence. At that time, he hadn't seen anything obsessive about her personality and told her so.

"I guess it only reveals itself when I'm in school or teaching. I used to take my job as a chemistry teacher far too seriously. I worked throughout summer vacations."

"How so, what did you do?"

"I planned labs, bought chemicals, organized the chemistry storeroom, while taking a couple of courses or workshops. I already had a master's degree in chemistry. I realize now I felt my ability was somewhat lacking, so I worked like hell to compensate."

"I bet you enjoyed working that hard."

She said smiling: "You're right. I did, but I didn't have enough time for family fun. Everything academic came so easily to Colton and Ralph."

This was when she told Greg about Madeira. "I wanted my students, all girls, of course, to consider careers in science. To do that, I had to set the example. After years of teaching high school chemistry, I started to feel comfortable, so I designed a course in planetary science for high school students, after having taken only one course in astronomy. I was never able to use the darn second-hand telescope I bought. Again, I was pushing myself beyond my ability."

Greg snapped out of these thoughts when Emily nudged him.

She was looking across the auditorium to her left. "Look over there. There's a woman with a dog in her lap. I hope it won't start barking. That could throw Colton off his track."

"They are allowing dogs to accompany people more now. They can be very comforting to their owners.... Wait a minute. I recognize that woman, I think." Greg stopped talking abruptly when he realized Colton was being introduced.

COLTON'S LECTURE

"Many of us are confused about just what is going on in Russia. Even those of us to whom Russia is the focus of our academic career are confused. So I'm going to start by covering some of the basic changes since the Soviet days.

"In 1988, when Mikhail Gorbachev became president, he changed Russia's course, directing it toward a democracy and a free economy. He knew the Cold War had had devastating effects on the Soviet economy. He wanted to ease restrictions, permit criticism of the communist government...glasnost... perestroika.... So you see, Gorbachev had no intention of ending the Soviet Union, he just wanted to take it in a new direction. He resigned in 1991.

"Boris Yeltsin won the election that followed. It was a legitimate election. It was never disputed that he had won the popular vote. Once in power, Yeltsin rapidly initiated even more changes. He immediately dissolved the Soviet Union and established the Russian Federation in its place. Russia and the other 14 Soviet Republics each became autonomous countries within that federation.

"Yeltsin then set out to convert a totalitarian communist society to a free market economy—a monumental task, I think you would agree. He tried to do it quickly, before entrenched conservatives had enough time to stop him. In his first year, he ended price subsidies and removed government controls of food and consumer goods.

"Most Russians were pleased with these changes, but the changes greatly reduced the government's source of revenue. Bankers loaned the government money with the stipulation that, if the government defaulted on the loans, the banks could sell government assets—state owned businesses. The government defaulted. Banks controlled the process that auctioned off the state's assets for much less than their value. The outcome was that a few people became very rich and the government was left significantly poorer. Critics referred to the rapid privatization as 'grabification;' economists as 'shock therapy.' You may have heard that term. In return for creating oligarchs, the oligarchs made sure Yeltsin was elected to a second term in 1996.

"Many of the Russian elites, the oligarchs, are ex-Soviet intelligence agents, like Putin. They stole through trickery many of Russia's state assets and are laundering their profits by investing in real estate in United States and Europe. This way, they avoid taxes. Our elites collude in their unethical activities by not insisting on transparency. Notice how much expensive property in New York, London, and Los Angeles is owned by Russians. We shouldn't take Russian elites for their word. They say they want a capitalist democracy, but by shadowing their thieving transactions, we are endangering our own democracy."

Colton paused to take a sip of water. So far, Greg thought Colton's lecture was interesting. Many parts he understood, but he wasn't clear on shock therapy. He smiled at Emily and gave her hand a squeeze. Her face revealed how pleased she was for her son.

Colton went on: "Yeltsin's dealings with Chechnya have been problematic. This is confusing. I will need to give you some background information. Chechnya is a small mountainous region in the Caucasus Mountains between the Caspian and the Black Seas. Russia had been trying to 'Russify' it for centuries. The Chechen people are ethnically distinct. They have a strong clan structure. There is little industrialization. The Chechen language is unrelated to Russian. Their religion is Islam.

"Chechnya seceded from the Russian Federation in 1991. Why did they want to be independent? It was not a recent aspiration. For centuries, Chechens wanted independence because Russia had felt threatened by having this strategic region populated by non-Russians.

"In 1944, for example, Stalin forcibly sent 500,000 Chechens to labor camps in Kazakhstan where 30% of them died. While the Chechens were in exile, tens of thousands of ethnic Russians were encouraged to move into Chechnya. Under the Khrushchev presidency, the surviving Chechens in Kazakhstan were allowed to return to Chechnya. Those returnees told about the horrors they had experienced, which added to two centuries of accumulated resentment. Chechens wanted out from under the Russian yoke.

"Yeltsin had many reasons for wanting to keep Chechnya within the Russian Federation. If one ethnic group seceded, an avalanche of others might follow. Also, Caspian Sea oil is refined in Baku, Azerbaijan and piped to Russia's Black Sea port of Novorossiysk. An independent Chechnya, Yeltsin thought, would put the pipeline in jeopardy. The huge Russian army no longer had a Soviet bloc to defend. It needed an excuse to perpetuate itself. Yeltsin thought he could gain popularity by a quick war in the south that would eliminate an unpleasant regime.

"The offensive was brutal and excessive. In 1994, Yeltsin ordered a huge number of Russian tanks and soldiers into Chechnya. Grozny, the capital of Chechnya, was leveled. The force was indiscriminate and disproportionate. Yet, Russian soldiers were ill-equipped, ill-trained, and couldn't effectively suppress Chechen rebels, who had resorted to guerilla warfare. A cease-fire was negotiated last year, and a peace treaty signed in May of this year.

"Despite the overwhelming advantage of the Russian Army in terms of manpower, weaponry, and airpower; its poor performance was demoralizing to Russians, and further eroded Yeltsin's declining popularity. A modest estimate suggests that 7,500 Russian troops and 50,000 Chechen civilians are dead, while an additional 500,000 Chechens have been displaced.

"The public became increasingly opposed to the war. Yeltsin

had a heart attack during his campaign for re-election. He would not have won without the illegal machinations of the oligarchs."

Greg was starting to doze off. When he came to, he realized Colton was concluding his lecture. Later, he would find out from Emily that he had slept through Colton's discussion of the Russian investigative journalist: Katya Drozdov. At least he heard Colton's summary.

"Shock therapy and the war in Chechnya have left the Russian people wondering where their country is going. It seems like the mob is in rule—mob in the sense of gangsters. The optimism that they felt at the beginning of the 1990s has greatly diminished. Russians are worried."

* * *

Greg and Emily joined the twenty or so people who moved close to the stage so they could ask Colton questions. Standing up to make this move, Greg looked for the woman with the dog. There she was, remaining in her seat, neither moving to the stage nor leaving. She seemed spellbound. Greg still could not place her, but he was sure he had seen her before. He couldn't ask Emily if she knew the woman—this was Emily's moment to relish Colton's glory.

Three weeks later, Greg saw the woman again, walking her dog around the lower lake. She was on the other side, so he couldn't get close to her, but he was sure it was the same woman.

Lena finally stood up and left the auditorium. As soon as she walked where there was grass, she let Laika down to pee. She was grateful that her little companion had been so good during the lecture. Back in her car, she had time to think. She thought she saw the policeman at the lecture, the man George played chess with, and evidently, the same man who had reprimanded Steve for making so much noise.

Lena knew Steve's work in the garage was noisy, but on the weekends, she went to the library or on frequent walks in various parts of the city. Balboa Park was her favorite. George said he hadn't realized the grinding noise lasted all day. He also spent much of the weekend away from home. Steve still didn't explain what he was doing, but made it very clear that Lena and George were not to go into the garage. Later, when George was alone with Lena, he asked her quietly: "Do you think Steve's strange behavior has anything to do with that woman he tries to see running around the lakes? Did you ever learn her name?"

"Hmm, I never thought of that...maybe...but I don't know who she is, either."

When the letter had come from the board, Lena and George were furious with Steve. How could he be so reckless? "Moscow, won't take this lightly," they told him. "In fact, to save your neck, we are going to have to pay for the changes to the house ourselves." When Steve realized the seriousness of the situation, he conceded to pay for half of both the electrical upgrade and air conditioning and all of the insulation expenses.

Lena kept sitting in her car. She wanted to think about what she had learned from Colton Dunn's lecture about Chechnya. She felt so fortunate that she had spotted the flyer advertizing it at the library. Their sleeper cell in Quietwater started in 1988. She knew about Gorbachev, but her knowledge of Yeltsin was sketchy and probably biased, as by this time, her sources of information came from the States, so she was glad to hear Dr. Dunn's analysis.

She didn't know that Chechens were tribal people, but she did know that they had resisted Russian dominance for years. She recalled what she had learned about her grandparents...the injustice of their suffering and dying in Kazakhstan. Whatever happened to them and to her parents, evidently, was not unusual. Dr. Dunn's lecture confirmed much of what she had read at the library.

Some things he said about the Chechen war were new to Lena. He said that the president of Chechnya was assassinated several months after the cease-fire. How unfair! The Russians must have tracked his location when he used his cell phone to make a call. Then they shot a missile at that location.

This was the very reason she kept her cell phone in a Faraday jacket. The importance of shielding your cell phone wasn't known a year ago when the president was assassinated. Then she thought about the new drone that General Atomics was in the early stages of designing. She didn't know much about it, except that it would be weaponized. She assumed that meant the drone could carry a missile on it, and that the same person directing its flight from the ground remotely could also fire the missile.

It occurred to her that the very technology she was stealing from General Atomics was helping Russians kill Chechens. She stopped breathing for a second or two. Was she betraying her own people? She didn't feel Chechen. She felt Russian. But she was Chechen. She thought she could remember people praying to Mecca when she was a child. Should she be an Islamist?

It was Saturday night, so she allowed herself a snack before going home. She stopped off at Rubio's and managed to get her order in just before closing. She ate the shrimp tacos in the car while thinking about her money situation. The cell didn't have a credit card. Each housemate had their own checking account. Each month, an equal amount of money was transferred from those three accounts to a pool account. The cell paid its bills from the pool account by an automatic debit system. There was no savings account. Moscow required that they keep their money only in checking accounts so they could get cash immediately if a hasty departure was required.

When she arrived home, neither George's nor Steve's car was in the driveway, but she parked in her usual spot on the street in front of the house anyway. As soon as she opened the car door, she heard the loud hum from the new air conditioner unit. It was located outside her window next to the front door, but behind bushes so it wasn't unsightly. Before it was installed, she used to wake up in the mornings to the clink-clink sound of the California Towhee, sometimes as early as 5:00 A.M., but now, if the air conditioner was left on all night, she couldn't hear much of the outdoors.

Both Steve and George had their bedrooms downstairs, so they couldn't hear the noise of the compressor's motor. George slept like a hibernating bear. Once he went to sleep, it was almost impossible to wake him.

Lena was exhausted. She took Laika out for her last pee and brought her into her bedroom for the night. The dog hopped up on the foot of the bed while Lena closed her curtains and got ready for bed. Lena propped both pillows up so she could read sitting up with her little nightlight on. She tried to become absorbed in the novel she was reading. It was no use, so she turned off the light and continued to think about Chechnya in the dark. After twenty minutes or so, she rearranged the pillows and lay down flat to go to sleep.

After a half hour, she heard a car drive up and recognized its chunking sound. "You've lost the packing grease on your CV joint," Steve had told George a couple of years ago. "You'd better get that fixed," George still hadn't fixed it. Ah yes, those are definitely George's footsteps—heavier than Steve's. She heard the TV. The volume was turned down, but Lena was sure George was listening to one of those political satire programs that come on after ten at night. He probably had Felice on his lap.

By the time Steve came home, Lena was getting upset with herself for not falling asleep. Steve's car motor was quiet, but his driving style was distinctive. A sudden stop was soon followed by the slamming of the car door. His footsteps were softer and quicker than George's. He usually wore trainers.

Lena finally went to sleep thinking about Colton Dunn's talk. Maybe he's someone she could talk to about Chechnya. UCSD wouldn't be likely to give out his address. Who was that Russian journalist he kept talking about? Tomorrow she'd go to the library and see if she could find any of her articles.

The next morning Lena slept later than usual, but it didn't matter. It was Sunday. She let Laika out the kitchen door that opened onto the deck overlooking the lower lake. Laika scooted down the steps from the deck to the backyard to do her business. What Laika did in the backyard didn't bother the men. Lena cleaned up after her fairly regularly. Steve never went in the backyard—never! Thank goodness. She emptied the last bit of dog food into Laika's dish and threw the can in the trash. It made a loud clank. Lena looked in the bin and confirmed her thoughts. Steve must have emptied the wastebasket from his room. There were at least three Vodka bottles. He did the bulk of his drinking on the weekends.

On her walks now, she made sure she had a note pad, pencil, and a small set of binoculars in the cloth bag she hung from her shoulder. Today, she took a sandwich with her, just in case she wanted to linger past her lunchtime. Off she went, letting Laika choose the direction.

At one point, they were on Aleppo Pine Drive. She saw ahead the junction box that she had walked into years ago. What's the word for the day? Bucolic—how appropriate! They walked past the house, when Laika emphatically reversed directions, forcing

Lena to turn around. There was a man bending over to pick up a newspaper. His shock of brown hair triggered a memory in Lena. As he stood up, she saw his dark bushy eyebrows and was astonished to recognize Dr. Colton Dunn. He lives in Quietwater! Why was Laika pulling on the leash trying to approach him? Lena thought it best to cover up her embarrassment by making a joke of the situation. "Laika just wanted to tell you that she enjoyed your lecture yesterday."

Colton walked over to the dog and bent over to pet her. "Laika, did you say?"

"Yes, Laika!"

He stood up and looked Lena in the eye. "A good Russian name. Are you Russian?"

"Nyet!" Oh my God, how could I have blurted that out with all the training I've had! She recovered by smiling. Hopefully, he'll think I was just being clever.

"Yet, you named your dog Laika. You must know the story."

She thought she had better continue the joke: "Dah."

Colton laughed and said to the dog: "Did you really go to my lecture yesterday?"

"Yes, she did. We enjoyed it very much." Colton kept looking at Lena. She added hesitantly: "I would love to know more about Chechnya." She probably shouldn't have said that.

"I can loan you a book, just a fascinating book…." He asked her to wait while he went inside to retrieve it.

They talked for a while. Lena thought she shouldn't borrow the book. She shouldn't get to know someone from the community, but she couldn't resist. She said she would have it back to him in a few days.

"You can have it if you want. I don't need it anymore," he offered.

"No, I'll return it in a few days. Thank you very much." She hurried off, pulling Laika along, afraid that he would ask where she lived or what her telephone number was.

Later that morning, walking on the footpath of the lower

lake, they neared the woods around a small parking lot. What the heck, nobody's around, why not let Laika have a run? At first, Laika meandered in her vicinity, but then she went into the bushes ahead. Lena noticed someone approaching on the path. "Laika…Laika." Where did she go? Then she saw Laika on an ill-defined path up the steep slope. She decided she would follow, to catch and leash her before she was sighted. There wasn't time, so she ducked behind a bush until the man went by.

By this time, Laika was 15 feet higher up the slope. Her little white head was tilted to one side. Her eyebrows were raised imploring Lena to do something. Do what? Laika wouldn't come down, so Lena managed to scramble up the cliff after her. She may be stuck, afraid to come down, or wants my company?

Her tail waged nonstop when Lena made it up the hill. Laika led her to the left to a little terrace, surrounded by bushes. There was an old lawn chair. Someone must have left it there years ago, now covered with cobwebs, dirt, and leaves. Lena set about cleaning it up as best she could before she tried to sit on it. She was prepared for it to collapse under her weight, but it didn't. In fact she felt quite secure sitting in it.

From where she sat she couldn't see the lake or the footpath around it. A few houses were visible, way up on the mesa. She looked through her binoculars. She wasn't familiar with any of those houses. To her delight, Laika had found her a little hideaway. It was private, pleasant, and quiet. She took out Colton's book from her bag, read a chapter, and then ate her sandwich. What a peaceful setting!

CANYONEER

A year ago, Emily had signed up for an extensive training course with San Diego's Natural History Museum. She was taught to lead hikes all over the county. As an amateur (very amateur!) naturalist, she was expected to know the native plants and animals common to each region of the county. The county was renowned for its biodiversity. She learned that there were five general habitats: sea coast, coastal plain (San Diego City), the foothills, the mountains, and the desert.

Upon passing the final test, Emily became a canyoneer. There were about 30 canyoneer hikes scheduled each week, covering all parts of the county. As a canyoneer, Emily was expected to lead or help lead at least one hike a week. Some were on Wednesdays, but most fell on Saturday and Sunday, when more people were off work. A few days in advance of leading a hike, Emily did a dry run so she would be sure to know the region's plants and special features that the trail offered. She was expected to know the geology and history as well as the plants and animals.

Emily, who had spent most of her life living on the East Coast, was in way over her head. It wasn't just that she was lacking in knowledge and experience, but she was 63 years old and was not in as good shape as she should be. Greg was always on her case to get more exercise. He was right.

She preferred to guide a group on Wednesdays, when few young people were off work. Climbing hills was difficult. Emily was often the last person to reach the top. When she got up there, the others were ready to move on and she hadn't recovered her breath or had the chance to tell them the story about the prickly pear and the cochineal insect.

Occasionally, she would knock on Colton's door to ask him to go with her. It would be good for him to get outside, get some exercise, and learn something about nature, she thought. Recently, she had been pleasantly surprised at his upbeat attitude.

"Hi, Mom, what's up?"

In fact, he was sounding downright cheery these days. Things must be going well for him at the university. Yet, when he heard her offer, he usually turned her down. The last time she asked, he leaned against the door frame, keeping a finger in a book to hold his place, and smiled at her patiently. She asked: "What are you reading?"

"Solzhenitsyn." He smiled again, then added, "*Gulag Archipelago.*"

Emily knew that by August, Colton usually started preparing for some seminar he would teach in the fall. "Are you going to be teaching Russian literature?"

"No, I'm just reading it for fun."

Fun! Oh well, she thought, and left him in peace, satisfied that at least he seemed happy, reading it for fun.

Spy Training

For her early morning walk, before she and Laika went to work, Lena preferred the footpath around the lakes. She knew Colton well enough now to know that he didn't spend time on his deck looking at people or the lakes, so she was confident he wouldn't see her. She didn't want him to realize that she lived in Quietwater.

She had become increasingly fond of this walk. There were arroyo willows in patches along the water's edge. Some branches bent over so far that their outermost leaves touched the water. They were long narrow leaves that fluttered with the slightest breeze, flashing silver on one side and glossy green on the other. It used to be that Lena's favorite trees were oaks, but now, she was no longer sure. She could relate to this tree's two personas and started to understand that its flexibility gave it strength.

Lena remembered when she first met Colton, how he asked if she knew the story about the dog Laika. Of course she knew it. No Russian could not know that story! Laika was the first living creature put into orbit around the Earth. Most Russians had a soft spot in their hearts for Laika, a mutt taken off the streets of Moscow, probably grateful to be fed while she was trained to accept being confined to a smaller and smaller space. She was spun in a centrifuge and learned to eat food in jelly form in preparation for her propaganda mission. The signals from Laika's heart and breathing monitors were lost 5-7 hours into the flight, so there was no electronic data concerning her death. Political pressure to celebrate the 40th anniversary of the Bolshevik Revolution was more important than devoting sufficient time to develop her life support systems.

Laika had all sorts of nicknames: Spacemutt, Sputmutt, dog cosmonaut.... Lena identified with Laika. They had a lot in common. She could be called Spymutt. The comparison led her to thoughts about how she was trained for espionage work.

They had been housed in a secret dacha outside of Moscow. It was furnished like an American home. They were given American clothes. She remembered her surprise that the shoes were so loose fitting—easily slipped in and out of. Thank goodness they didn't force her to take up smoking. In every room there were tape recorders running, broadcasting the American news. They were expected to browse newspapers and magazines and encouraged to look at American movies. There were videos of American TV shows as well as films specially designed to educate them, not just in American history and culture, but about details like typical days at school at a variety of grade levels. Their teachers were former illegals themselves, with reasonable American accents.

Within a month of arriving at the dacha, Lena was sent to an orthodontist to get her teeth straightened. Lena wasn't expected to know as much about sports as the male agents, but she had to know how to set a table, to cook typical American meals, and be familiar with common snacks. The training went on for two years, from 1986 to 1988. They were supposed to resist talking to the other trainees, and if they did, they were told to always speak in English. Once they were located in the States, the books in their home should all be in English. Lena was taught to drive a car. She even had to attend a university in Canada for a semester before the move to San Diego.

She was amazed that Russia invested so much in a sleeper cell: their training, renting a home for them in San Diego, as well as buying three secondhand cars. This initial investment came when the USSR was suffering serious financial difficulties. Did they feel they needed more presence in the USA's Navy hub on the West Coast?

She remembered that while they were being trained in

Moscow, they were shown a 1980 Soviet map of San Diego naval facilities: submarine base, a naval airbase, ammunition depots, and factories that made aircraft and weapons. Along with the map were notes on public transportation, communications systems, and the height and architecture of buildings in various parts of town.

This map generated a long discussion about the Russian military mapping program. Lena and the other trainees learned about the tens of thousands of Russian surveyors and topographers who gathered data in the field, and the hundreds of Russian cartographers who compiled these data to make the maps. The trainees were shown some of the other maps. They were truly impressive.

"You are probably wondering why we bothered mapping the world in such detail," a trainer said to them. His next statement shocked Lena. "The U.S. military has air superiority over Russia." Such a frank admission was rare during the Cold War. Perhaps, they figured we would learn that once we started living in San Diego, she reasoned.

The trainer went on to explain that as a result of that superiority, U.S. maps only recorded medium scale details. "We Russians, on the other hand, are leaders in tank technology, and since World War II, we have built up the most powerful army in the world. We need maps to help us maneuver our large army and its tanks. Our maps have to be more detailed. We have mapped almost the entire world in magnificent detail. No matter where our military finds itself on the ground, we will know how to go from point A to point B."

Lena returned to her original question: why did Russia bother with sleeper cells? Like its map strategy, Russia was planning years ahead. She learned that the first generation of the sleeper agents were not required to penetrate the target country's government or intelligence. George and Steve are living the typical life of the first generation illegals, she thought. She, on the other hand, was lucky to get her job at General Atomics, but unlucky in that Moscow couldn't resist taking advantage of her position with the company. She was given an assignment in her first year as an agent.

General Atomics periodically gave its employees pep talks. It told them how good GA products were, how the company was on the cutting edge of technology, how although Russia had developed complex air and space systems, it was not competent in designing and producing UAVs (unmanned aerial vehicles, ie., drones). According to one pep talk, by the end of the Cold War, Russia's economy was so depressed it couldn't afford to develop the optics or electronics for light aircraft.

That was probably true, Lena thought, but there was more to the story. She knew that Russia's huge landmass originally discouraged the government's pursuit of drone technology. Most Americans can't comprehend that Russia has over 13 thousand miles of land borders and 23 thousand miles of coastline to protect. So far, drones developed elsewhere could not cope with Russia's harsh winters, especially in the northern regions where fog, rain, and snow are frequent. However, as Colton pointed out in his lecture, drones served Russia well in the Caucasus during the Chechen war, where the opponents, the Chechens, were much weaker militarily.

The first application of drones that Russia found helpful was short-range surveillance. Later, they learned how to guide and fire a ground-based missile at a target identified by a drone's camera. This allowed both Russia and the U.S. to assassinate enemy leaders with impunity. Now that drones themselves could be weaponized, Russia's interest in drone technology had increased significantly.

Lena knew that the company she worked for, General Atomics, was designing a new drone, or possibly a much-advanced version of an old drone. She heard engineers talking excitably about the P1. They moved between each other's offices quicker than usual, speaking in hushed tones. Gabriella, who often cracked jokes at a fast clip, was quieter than usual. She seemed intensely serious. Gabriella was young, good looking, and smart. Actually they were all smart. That was one reason Lena loved working at General Atomics.

Another reason, trivial maybe, was they were casually dressed. She could go from her early morning walk straight to work, without having to change clothes. A third reason was that so many of her cohorts were foreign born. In front of them she didn't feel the need to act so American. She didn't have to speak louder than she wanted or overdo the smiling and laughing. All of these things made Lena feel more comfortable. Gabriella herself was Italian. Something about her was nagging Lena, but she couldn't figure out what it was.

Lena had been promoted several times since General Atomics hired her ten years prior. She now had the opportunity to steal something important—the pre-programmed software for the Predator drone. She heard rumors that each Predator drone would cost $11 million.

Did she really want to steal it? She had no choice. That was Moscow's mission for her. If she refused to complete her mission, the Kremlin would have her terminated. She knew too much. She couldn't even let on that the mission made her uncomfortable. Then they would fear she might defect. Defection would be far worse for Moscow than quitting. She could divulge so much vital information to the Americans.

She forced herself to contemplate happier thoughts—reading books together with Colton. She had almost finished the latest one that he had loaned her: Pushkin's *Eugene Onegin*, a love story written in verse. By now, she no longer pretended she was not Russian, but she still refused to tell him her last name or where she lived. Once he accepted that rule, they thoroughly enjoyed their discussions together. It was so wonderful to have a true friend.

They often talked of Chechnya and commiserated on the conditions of daily life there. She asked him if he knew about the Chechen surgeon—Baiev Khassen—who once, in a 48-

hour period, had performed sixty-seven amputations and eight brain surgeries in Grozny. "Oh yes," he answered. "He was the only surgeon for the 80,000 residents of Grozny. Such terrible conditions!"

She gave Colton her cell phone number. It couldn't be traced. By this time, they were getting together once a week. He had to call her to set up the time. She didn't know his number. Today, they were going to the Timken Museum to see the Russian icons.

Oktoberfest 2000

Outside the community room where the HOA board meetings were held was a large terrace area under a pergola. The swimming pool and tennis courts were nearby, but on this day in late October, all activity was on the terrace. Tables, as many as 15, were set up and covered with plastic tablecloths. Grills were fired up, big aluminum serving dishes were kept warm by hot water. There were special tables for casseroles and salads and another for desserts. Beer kegs, wine, and soft drinks were in coolers at the other end of the terrace. A bouncy castle was set up in the parking lot for the kids.

Greg was hanging a piñata. "That's too high," Emily said.

"Yes, high now…can walk under it…lower it when the time comes."

He never completes his sentences these days. He has a lot on his mind, she thought. It was time for her to go home and fetch her casserole, cork screw, and what else? Oh yes, Colton.

Later, Emily, with plate full, looked for a place to sit down. She chose a table where there were some people she knew and some she didn't know. Getting to know your neighbors in the Quietwater community—that was what Oktoberfest was all about. She wished Greg could settle down and sit with her, but he had responsibilities.

After finishing her food and chatting with her neighbors, she began to wonder where Colton was. Ah, over there standing all alone next to a water dish put out for dogs. She walked up to him with the intent of inviting him to sit with her.

"Hi, I just heard from Katya," he told her.

"Katya Drozdov?"

"Yes, her husband was in the Kurst submarine."

Emily had to think a minute. Is this something she should know? "The what?"

"Mom, you know the submarine that sank a month-and-a-half ago in the Barents Sea? Remember, it was a nuclear submarine? Remember, Putin was staying in a resort? Remember, he delayed accepting foreign help and then, when they tried to rescue the sailors, it was too late?"

"Oh, oh yes, that was tragic! My goodness, yes, I'm so sorry. She lost her husband, you said?"

"That may be why I haven't heard from her in so long."

Colton took Katya's letter out from his shirt pocket. Why did he bring it here to Oktoberfest? He knows I can't read Russian. "Oh, yes...it's coming back to me. The boat was just resting on the sea floor, not very far from the surface as I recall. So terrible to know they were alive and yet nothing was done to save them for days. Didn't everyone die?"

"Yes, eventually. All 118 men. Sergei was one of the officers. Katya says the crew was inexperienced and had not been trained adequately. They were even using a manual for another ship. I'll tell you more about it when we're home."

"Have you said hello to Greg? He could probably use some help with something." Colton started looking around. She followed where he was looking and spotted a friend. "Oh I'd like you to meet my friend, Yvonne, over there."

"Mom, if you don't mind, I want to get back home."

"OK, dear. Will this change your plans about going to Russia? I know you were planning on staying with Katya."

"No, it doesn't, but I want to send her a letter today."

"Why don't you just call her?"

"She says I shouldn't do that." He paused to look around again. "This is a good turnout, isn't it? ...Well, see you back at the house."

For a minute, Emily was saddened by Colton's lack of

sociability. He was a good person, but just didn't seem to need people. She went to find Greg. He was setting the right height for the piñata. The children were waiting eagerly. Greg was enjoying himself.

Meteor Shower

Almost a year later, August 12 was a hot night. Emily desperately tried to go to sleep. She had set the alarm for 2:00 A.M. so she could get up to see the Perseid Meteor Shower. The shower happened every year at this time, but this year it was to come closely after a new moon, when the night sky is darkest. This year, the shower should be spectacular. She planned to go out on her deck that overlooked the lower lake. At that hour, everybody in Quietwater should be sound asleep with their lights out.

Emily had hoped Greg would join her. Before she called to ask him, she quickly reviewed what her astronomy book said. She knew these shooting stars would have theoretically originated in the Perseid constellation, but she could never find that constellation. What causes them? Greg would want to know. Emily consulted her old astronomy book: Meteor showers happen when Earth passes through the debris field of a comet or asteroid as these objects make their way around the sun, shedding 'crumbs' along the way.

When Emily asked Greg if he wanted to join her, he declined, muttering that he had to get to sleep because of the fish! It sounded like he was already half asleep. What did fish have to do with it? Oh well.

She had brought another fan in from the garage and placed it so that its breeze was aimed at her in bed. Should she drag out her telescope? It always took her 15 minutes to get the darn thing pointing in the right direction. Actually, the shower covered such a wide area in the sky there would be no point in trying to use it, unless she wanted to take a look at the moon. But then she remembered, it was a new moon just two days ago. Tonight, only a toenail would be lit up. Which way would the toenail be opening up? Oh, give it up and just go to sleep, she told herself. She'd just use her binoculars.

The alarm did awaken her, so she must have fallen asleep. Rousing herself was not easy, but by the time she was out on the deck, her enthusiasm had returned. The temperature was about 70°F, perfect! She took her time to adjust her eyes to the dark night sky. Thirty minutes minimum is what astronomers recommend. She opened up a lounge chair so she could lie down flat, thereby taking in as much of the night's sky as possible. She tried not to think of the spiders who worked diligently all night long, spinning their webs. They loved lawn chairs.

There were few clouds. Within ten minutes of just lying there, she saw a streak in the sky that quickly disappeared. A minute later there was another, then another. Then, something flew across her line of vision that was close. It frightened her. It was too big to be a bat or a bird. She sat up and tried to find it. There it is. She saw it in the distance whizz up higher and go over the mesa out of sight. She waited, thinking it might return. After ten minutes, she grew impatient, and lay down again to concentrate on spotting more shooting stars.

She saw a few more, but wished Greg was with her. She was uncomfortable and felt exposed. Finally, she had had enough. She checked out the moon's toenail and justified to her satisfaction the way it opened up. She went back into the dark house and found her way to her bedroom. For once, she had no trouble falling asleep.

She called Greg first thing in the morning, but he didn't answer. He's out jogging she thought. After waiting 40 minutes, he still didn't answer. Emily thought of the woman the board members jokingly referred to as UFO. Emily knew her real name was Ebony Harris and that she lived next door to Joan, a woman with whom she occasionally went bird-watching. She wanted to compare her experience with those of Ebony's. It must be a drone, Emily surmised. She had heard about drones on the news. She drove to Ebony's house because she lived on the other side of Quietwater and she didn't know her phone number.

Fish Kill

When Emily finally got through to Greg on the phone, he asked: "Have you been down to the lakes?"

"Not for a couple of days."

"Come down. I'll meet you at the lower lake at the little parking lot."

Emily walked with Greg on the footpath. There were a few fish turned on their sides floating on the surface, obviously dead.

"What has happened?"

"We don't know. We've had two companies come out this morning to take samples of the water."

"Is the upper lake affected as well?"

"Yes, sure. The water is circulated from one lake to the other. You can hear the pump. We run it 12 hours during the day. So whatever affects one lake will eventually affect the other."

"This is terrible."

"You're telling me."

"Do you think someone put poison in the water, maybe one of those boys who tries to fish here? Over the years we've run off several people." She wasn't thinking very clearly. Quietwater had put up several signs that said: "No Fishing." From her deck, she had shouted at people when she saw them starting to fish, ignoring the signs. Emily remembered a red-haired boy who rode his bike in with a fishing pole strapped to his back. It did look like fun, she had to admit. Nonetheless, she diligently shooed him away as many as three times over the years.

"Yeah, there are lots of people we have had to ask to leave in spite of the 'No Trespassing' signs everywhere. I'm not looking forward to the board meeting tomorrow night."

* * *

Ebony had not been home, so Emily still hadn't had the chance to confer with her about the 'UFO.' Greg was completely preoccupied by the dead fish, and Colton, with Russia. Although she was disappointed, she hadn't been able to impress anybody with her previous night's adventure, she could at least be supportive of Greg and go to the board meeting.

There were only three seats left when Emily walked in during the public comment session. Opinions and complaints were non-ending:

"The turtles haven't died because they're herbivores."

"No, I saw a turtle eat a duckling."

"There are no ducklings because there are so few ducks."

The general consensus was that everybody missed the ducks. Someone said that she hadn't seen an osprey for two years. Others said they were sorry the turtles weren't affected—Quietwater had far too many turtles. Another said that if we allowed dogs to be off leash that would take care of the turtle problem. "I object," a little old lady said. "Turtles should not be seen as a problem. Why are they considered inferior to fish?"

President Marco Romero said that the results of the testing would take another week, at least.

"In a week they'll all be dead," said Aaron Goldfarb storming out of the meeting.

"Without our lakes our community is nothing."

"Please wait to be called on," the president said. "Ebony, you've been waiting patiently. What did you want to say?"

"I saw it again, flying over the canyon." Suppressed chuckles lowered the tension in the room.

"What time?" Emily blurted out. She heard a woman seated close by whisper: "Don't encourage the nutcase." Greg did not looked pleased with her for speaking without being called on.

"Between 2:30 and 3:30 A.M. I was looking at the meteor shower when it flew by."

"I saw it too," Emily said. "Could it be a drone?"

"Dead fish and an aerial attack. We have problems," Marco said, smiling. "Yes, Morgan, do you have a comment. This will have to be our last."

"Yes, the other night, I was looking through my notebook and read about Mr. Thornpeck's complaint in July of 1995, that his roses were snipped off by someone in the middle of the night, just when they were in full bloom. The board never reported back to us about that. Perhaps that same person killed the fish."

"Thank you Morgan. The vandalism of Mr. Thornpeck's roses was, fortunately, a one-off. Well, we have to close the public comment session and go into our regular meeting. We have a lot of business we have to attend to."

Emily caught up with Ebony on leaving the meeting. They compared notes. Both agreed it was a drone that they had seen. "But why fly it at night? Why not during the day?" They exchanged telephone numbers. Ebony suggested that they go together to next month's gathering of the amateur astronomy society out in the Laguna Mountains. "Do you have a telescope?" Emily delayed answering, so Ebony continued: "Not to worry, several people come with fantastic equipment and they love to share."

General Atomics

Art Campbell, Gabriella Rossi, several other design engineers, and Vice President and Controller of General Atomics Carmichael met with a top CIA director, James Woolsey, to discuss the CIA's desire to contract for a more advanced drone.

Mr. Woolsey explained why the CIA was interested in General Atomics' latest drone: "We have slain a large dragon. But we live now in a jungle filled with a bewildering variety of poisonous snakes. And in many ways, the dragon was easier to keep track of."

Snakes and a dragon—what is the man talking about? They finally realized he was referring to the breakup of the Soviet Union, and that gathering intelligence via satellite was no longer adequate. Satellites limited surveillance to just a few minutes each day. Drones had proven efficient. They could loiter over a conflict area for close to twenty hours at a time. Now, the United States had to keep tabs on several new nations as well as other regions clamoring for independence. To this end, the CIA had already contracted with General Atomics to purchase their Gnat-750 drone.

To acquire yet another contract with the CIA, Woolsey insisted that GA tighten its security. For years, there had been armed guards at the front gates. Occasionally, the cars of employees were checked before passing through the entrance gates to the parking lot. If there had been a recent terrorist threat, Lena's car was often searched. She, like other employees, had a radio frequency identification badge (RF-ID) to allow her to enter specific buildings.

It appeared that Woolsey was close to insisting on having X-ray machines installed. "We are 10-15 years ahead of those Ruskies. Let's keep it that way."

Word got around about Woolsey's threat. By that time, Lena had already been bringing Laika with her to work every day. She thought she had better be prepared for the day that they checked purses and brief cases. She wondered if Woolsey had been informed about Laika. The dog's name alone could have set off alarm bells in him.

Lena had to plan how she was going to be able to sneak in and out with her flash drive. She decided to glue a strip of Velcro on the inside of Laika's collar and the other piece of Velcro she glued to the flash drive. She left it attached to the collar at all times so Laika would get used to it. Laika always wore her collar.

Lena was particularly nervous about her next theft. Now, she was up against somebody who was an expert in spy matters. Woolsey's security audit team advised them all how to be on their guard, and what sorts of things they should look out for.

What Lena didn't know was that cameras had also been installed in every office with a computer storing the latest code. CIA people put the cameras in over a weekend so none of the employees would be aware that they were being watched. The cameras were cleverly concealed in the air conditioning vents. Each office had two vents, allowing the filming to cover most of the office space.

Lena always had plenty of work to do. She had less-strategic programs to debug beside the drone work. She helped to improve communications within the company, and suggested ways to alter other programs that had nothing to do with drones, to make them more efficient. All the time, she looked for opportunities to steal the latest package.

When she realized that she had not been asked to work on P1 for over a month, Lena figured the company was probably testing their latest prototype in the field. She kept waiting for an opportunity to steal the package. The day came when she noticed

Art, her boss, take an early lunch. She couldn't believe her luck as he had left his door open. Lena removed the flash drive from Laika's collar and left her office closing her door behind her. She put on a plastic glove and quietly slipped into Art's office. She was just about to insert her flash drive when she heard the bubbly voice of Gabriella in the far distance. She quickly left Art's office with her heart beating frantically and made her way to the woman's restroom. She averted that disaster, but for the rest of the day, she couldn't remain calm or recover her ability to concentrate.

Another opportunity did not occur for three weeks. This time, she was successful and it went like clockwork. She got back in her own office, shut the door, and stuck the flash drive to Laika's collar. Only then did her hand stop shaking.

When Lena got home, it was too dark to dead drop the package. There was no way she could pretend to look for a book at the Little Library in the dark. She poured herself a glass of wine and sat down in the living room to relax.

"Would you like me to go to Rubio's for take out?"

Lena couldn't believe her ears. Was that Steve she was hearing, offering to do something for her? Her face must have revealed her thoughts.

"Well, I can see you're tired. I'd like to go for Rubio's, if you don't want to cook. I love their California bowl. What about you, George?"

"Yeah, sure. Get me the fish taco plate that comes with chips."

"Great, then I'll take the usual: the shrimp taco platter for me. Thanks." Lena went into her bedroom with Laika and removed the flash drive from her dog's collar, put it in her purse, and went back in the living room to finish her wine. Perhaps tonight she would have another glass. Tomorrow morning she would put the package at the dead drop before going to work.

The dead drop was the Little Library on Scott Street, a short side street several blocks away from Quietwater. The Little Library itself was just a cabinet with two shelves and a glass door, supported by a post in the ground. Anybody from anywhere could leave off or take a book from it. It was totally free. If you took a book, you didn't have to return it.

It made for an ideal dead drop. It was not that easily seen because it was surrounded on three sides by tall bushes and located on a vacant lot. Since you didn't have to be from that neighborhood in order to use it, nobody walking up to it would appear suspicious.

This was the fourth time she had used this dead drop. In the morning she walked from home carrying a book. She opened the door and browsed the books available. Once she was sure she was alone, she taped the flash drive to the outside bottom of the cabinet. She looked at several books, selected one, and walked back home. She then drove to work making sure she got there on time.

After work, Lena drove home, picked up her burner phone in its Faraday jacket, and walked to the bus stop. She took a bus to National City. She got off the bus and walked a few blocks away from the stop before she took out her phone and sent her handler the text message: *The chicken is done and out of the oven.* She quickly put the phone back in the Faraday jacket so as to minimize the time her position could be located. Then she returned by bus to Quietwater.

A week later, as soon as Lena entered the GA building, two muscular armed guards walked up to her and asked her to follow them. She was escorted to the office of the vice president and controller who dismissed her from her duties at General Atomics. She gave the guards her RF-ID which had already been deactivated. When she asked Mr. Carmichael why she was being dismissed, he merely nodded to the guards to take her away. Her arms were held firmly and she was escorted to her office. Still on her leash, Laika growled softly. Lena said: "That's all right, Laika." It seemed that people closed the doors to their offices as she passed by, or was she just anticipating the scorn that she knew she deserved? She had one minute to gather up her belongings before she was escorted out of the building. No one said goodbye.

She had imagined this moment many times. It was what she had always dreaded the most, but she had assumed the police would be present, that she would be arrested and taken to jail. After that, someone from the Russian Embassy would come and negotiations would start from there. Her story about being a stray, a pawn in the hands of others, would come out in the newspapers, or at least in some report.

Instead, she was simply thrown out and would never be allowed back in. She felt shabby, dirty, and unwanted again. She had been deceitful to people who had been nice to her, and now she couldn't even say goodbye or explain to them why she had lied to them.

It was Colton she regretted disappointing the most. He loved Russia. They both loved the same things about Russia, not the politics, but its magnificent culture. Over the last year, he had been educating and exposing her to its rich beauties.

She went home. Her housemates were out at work. She had all day to stew about why General Atomics didn't call the police. Does that mean they weren't going to press charges? And how did they find out what she had been up to? Why did Mr. Carmichael not even give her a reason why she was fired? Where had she gone wrong?

She waited until both George and Steve were home before she broke the news. They both looked sick. "Maybe they'll come for all of us," George said.

"Who, the police?" Steve asked.

"Who else? Of course the police!"

Lena watched Steve. She had never seen him scared before. She resented his careless, thoughtless, behavior in the past that had come so close to exposing them all. Anger welled up in her as she recalled his drinking and violent tantrums. Lena went on the attack. "What have you been working on in the garage?" When he didn't respond, she knew it was trouble. She looked at George.

"Come on," George said. "We have to know now." He got up

and started walking to the garage door.

"OK, I've been making drones."

"Drones, why?"

By this time George had opened the door from the hall that led to the garage. He stepped inside. Lena was right behind him. There, they saw three drones, each no bigger than four feet across. "Why have you been making these?" (No answer.) "Why the secrecy?"

Steve looked at Lena. "Oh, I was just having a little fun."

"Why couldn't you tell us what you were doing?"

"You'd laugh at me. I was afraid you would make me stop, and say that I shouldn't do what I did with them."

"Good grief, what did you do with them?" George was getting mad, too. That was something Lena had never seen.

"She didn't know it was me."

"Who?"

"Oh, you know—Gabriella. At first I tried to make a drone to deliver things to her."

"Good heavens! That same neighborhood jogger? What did you try to deliver?"

"Just rose petals, because they were lightweight."

"What? You risked exposing our cell to deliver rose petals?" Lena was about to explode. All this time, the woman Steve had a crush on was her co-worker! Had GA fired her because of Steve? That was where her thoughts were going.

"No, no, she doesn't know it was me. She hardly knows I exist, yet."

"Yet! What in hell were you planning to do?" George asked.

"I just flew my first drone over her house and dropped rose petals on her front doorstep. That's all."

"What? When did you do that?"

"A long time ago, but then I realized I had a much better way of making drones. I've designed them to take off vertically. They run on an electric battery, and maneuver more like a helicopter."

Lena was overwhelmed, both furious with Steve, and yet

impressed with his creativity.

"I think General Atomics and others are stuck with the concept that a drone should mimic an airplane, you know, by having fixed wings. Vertical takeoffs are much more practical. At some point, I guess I thought I'd show one to her, maybe, but I knew you wouldn't approve…"

Lena looked at George and saw from his facial expression that he was as amazed as she was. They knew Steve was bright, but this was unexpectedly outstanding, although completely inappropriate. Over the next hour, they extracted the full explanation from Steve. Evidently, he only made that one delivery to Gabriella Rossi. After that, he became much more interested in designing drones. He mostly tested them out in the desert. Only occasionally did he fly them in the wee hours of the morning from the back deck of their home.

"It wasn't dangerous," Steve explained, "the developer put all the electrical wires to people's homes underground here."

"But you were taking a risk. Anyone could have seen you."

"Not at that time of night!"

"There's always someone who is up. We're supposed to keep a low profile. That's the first thing they taught us. I must say, however, Steve, your invention is remarkable."

"Yes, indeed," George said, "but," he hesitated, "just because the police didn't arrest you on your job, Lena, doesn't mean they won't do it. They know where you live. They could come first thing in the morning."

"Let's think this through. What's the best thing for us to do right now?"

"If the police come and find the drones here, General Atomics will take credit for my discovery because I'm one of their employees. That would mean the technology would be American property," said Steve.

"Wait a minute! I thought you worked for 21st Century Technology."

"I do," he said, "but 21st is a subsidiary of General Atomics."

Lena realized that the misconception came about because she and Steve never talked much, and here they were housemates!

"If the police came and only arrested me on a charge of espionage, they would pursue the investigation until they found the Russia connection," Lena said. "Would Russia claim us?"

"Yes, I think they would," George said. "We'd be swapped, maybe. In any case, we'd end up living in Russia." There was silence. Nobody was smiling. George went on to say: "For now, it's best if we hide the drones."

"Our family will appear kooky. Once they become skeptical about our relationships, they may dig up who we really are. It's either prison here or return to Russia."

"I say we get rid of the drones right now, but could you recreate their specifications, when we've made contact with Russia?" George asked Steve.

"Easily! My brain is hard-wired with them. OK, if we have to hide them, let's give them a Viking burial. I've always wanted to do that."

"How so?" asked Lena. Steve's answer confirmed what she had always thought about him—he was a brilliant 31-year-old with the maturity level of a teenager.

They went to bed and set their alarms. None of them slept well. In the dark, Steve brought his three drones up to the deck. At 2:00 A.M., George and Lena stumbled out in their pajamas and sat down, ready to witness the burial. Nobody spoke. Steve seemed to know exactly what he was doing. He told them to move their chairs back, next to the banister.

He fiddled with the drone he had placed in the middle of the deck. "Just sit still," he whispered to them and went back into the garage to fetch his laptop. Keying in to his computer took five minutes. Then the drone rose straight up 200 feet in the air. It moved horizontally and hovered over the lake. All of the sudden, it appeared to fall down at top speed and splashed out of sight. Steve grinned and then clapped silently with boyish joy that was contagious.

In an hour's time, the other two drones were at the bottom of the lower lake as well. The three of them went into the living room but didn't turn on the lights. George said to Steve: "Now we have to straighten out the garage so there is as little evidence as possible of what you've been up to."

Steve quietly deposited his flash drives, manuals and books about drones into their next door neighbor's trash bin. Thank goodness the Offenbachers didn't wake up.

To help Steve, Lena and George shined a flashlight whenever he couldn't see what he had to do. The machinery was moved to the side of the garage and put on shelves. Thin sheets of aluminum were lifted up high and put in the rafters. In the space that was cleared, Steve parked his car.

That job finished, they sat in the living room to discuss their situation further. "They probably had you on camera, Lena," George said. "That would give General Atomics the proof they needed to justify firing you. They didn't confront you. Even the guards didn't seem to know why you were fired. They passed up the opportunity to see you squirm or to try to get you to divulge who your sponsor was. They decided not to bring in the police because they left your seizure up to the company's guards. Why wouldn't they want the police involved?"

They considered George's comments in silence, before he continued, "Bad publicity. Nobody wants to do business with a company that cannot secure their products."

Lena rushed in to say: "Yes, that's it! Many of General Atomics' clients are military. The military wants to be sure their adversaries can't get the product." There was silence again while the three of them were deep in thought. "I'll have to let Moscow know I was fired. You know, the package was so easy to take this time, I wonder if they set it all up." Again they were quiet. Lena suddenly realized she was tired. They all looked tired. "I wonder if the package was a phony. If so, what will Moscow do?"

"Nothing, they'll do nothing. They don't want to expose our sleeper cell, if at all possible. Everything will go on as usual, only you, Lena, will not have a job."

Lena thought to herself that not only will she not have a job, she could no longer be a Russian agent.

George looked up at the ceiling and mumbled: "He probably didn't want to accuse you of industrial espionage in front of the guards. Mr. Carmichael, is that his name? He wouldn't want GA clients to know there had been a breach in security."

Lena saw why Moscow put George in the sleeper cell. He could think clearly under stress and make a reasonable analysis. By the time they went to bed, it was five in the morning. The two men only caught a couple of hours of sleep. Lena had trouble falling asleep, but once she did, she didn't wake up until late in the morning. It didn't matter. She had no job to go to.

OKTOBERFEST 2001

Oktoberfest had come around again. Emily greeted some people she knew at the casserole table. Once her plate was loaded, she joined a group seated at a table nearby, not realizing that there was a heated discussion going on. She said hello. Someone introduced her to the others at the table. Their discussion quickly resumed.

"They should place more plants in the lakes. Plants filter out the impurities."

"That won't take care of the golden algae."

"Are they sure it is golden algae? They're not really sure that was what killed the fish, are they?"

"This board doesn't know what they are doing."

Emily's two acquaintances at the table looked embarrassed for her and gave her a slight smile. They don't know what to say, Emily thought. After all, she and Greg were not married and didn't even live in the same house.

"Without the lakes, this place is just like any other HOA community. The lakes are what make it special."

"Then there's the problem of the lining. Have you heard about that?"

Emily got distracted looking at the man at the end of the table, who had been introduced to her as George. She wondered if he was the same George that Greg played chess with. He didn't look very well, she thought, before she tuned back into the conversation again.

"You mean if they have to drain the lakes?"

"Yes, evidently new linings for both lakes would cost over

$300,000. And they only have $230,000 in the reserves designated for lake linings."

"Could they use the lake water for irrigation? That would save money. What a shame to put all that water down the storm drains."

"I don't remember, either we can't put the water down the storm drains or we can, but the city will charge us an arm and a leg for doing so."

At this point, Emily wished she could move to another table, not that she wasn't interested in the lakes. Ah, there was her excuse. Colton was helping himself to a bratwurst. She was so glad he had decided to join the party. He was looking around. He's probably looking for me, she thought so she stood up and waved him over. He smiled at her, but continued to survey the people. She was a little embarrassed, so she sat down again at the table. A couple of people had moved off, but their seats were taken by another couple she didn't know. The conversation continued.

"I was asked to test the water on goldfish. I had two buckets, one with lake water and the other with dechlorinated tap water. The fish in the lake water were dead in 15 minutes."

"Someone on the board suggested treating the lake water with charcoal. The water could be forced to run through a charcoal filter in the streambed connecting the two lakes. The water is circulated between the lakes. That's why the pump at the lower lake makes so much damn noise."

Emily noticed that George had left. The couple who had just sat down was eager to continue the topic."What about that woman who's a marine biologist? She seemed to really know her stuff."

"Yes, but she's too scientific for some to understand what she says. Besides, she refuses to get rid of the dandelions in her lawn. Yeah, they're all weird. We need a new board."

Emily got up and said with a smile: "The board members are all volunteers, you know. They are not paid. It's good that we all take a strong interest in the lakes. Maybe one of us will volunteer to be a board member next April, when the elections come up." Nobody responded. "Well, time for something sweet." She moved off to the dessert table.

Rain

Colton gave another lecture at UCSD in January, 2002. This one explained how Putin rose to power and initiated the second Chechen war. His talk highlighted Katya Drozdov as a war correspondent for the newspaper *Novaya Gazeta*.

Driving home from the lecture, Greg wanted to be sure he had understood some things Colton had said. "Let's see…so Yeltsin was unpopular for both losing the first Chechen war and the killing of so many Chechen civilians. Was it 30,000 civilians who were killed?"

"More like 80,000," Emily corrected him.

"And then, Yeltsin turned over the reins to Putin…."

"They made a deal, as I understand it. Yeltsin made Putin his prime minister and, a little later, wanted Putin to succeed him as president," Emily said. "In return, Putin made sure the charges against Yeltsin were dropped." They were both silent thinking about that. Then Emily went on to say: "Colton has told me several times about the mess Chechnya was in after that first war. He actually saw the devastation firsthand. He went to Grozny with Katya. Evidently, the capital was totally destroyed, the economy, too. Warlords tried to take over the government."

"Didn't Colton say: 'Chechen men were unemployed and had guns?'"

"Yes, and that some Chechens were starting to collaborate with the Taliban."

"OK, I remember him saying that Islamic extremists started exploiting the situation by introducing Sharia. That's what they call it, don't they, their system of law…medieval?"

"Yes, yes, terrible! Now tell me about the apartment bombings. I'm not sure I got that, you know...in Moscow?" Emily asked.

"As I understood it," Greg answered, "Putin blamed the bombings on Chechen terrorists. That gave him an excuse to start another war with Chechnya and made him popular with Russians. So they elected him president."

"Colton said that Katya published evidence implying Putin's government was complicit with the bombing. As Colton says— she's a fearless truth teller!"

"So, to put it crudely: Putin killed Russians sleeping in their apartments at night and blamed it on the Chechens. This gave him an excuse to start a second war in Chechnya. Russians were glad he was going to take down the Chechens so they approved of the war and elected him president."

"Yes. Thank goodness there are still some newspapers that are not controlled by the Kremlin. Colton fears that under Putin's presidency, some of the worst aspects of the Soviet Union have been revived." She wondered if this is what was making Colton so glum these days.

When they got back to Emily's house, Greg came in for a glass of wine. Colton was being taken out to dinner by his department at the university.

As soon as they were in the house it started to rain. Rain was always so welcomed in San Diego. The city got little more than 10" of rainfall a year. What rain it did get usually came in November through January. It was the only time of year when a person's skin wasn't flaky and the hills were green. The refreshing smell of sage and eucalyptus filled households. It was too dark to see the lake at this time of night, but maybe the rain would last into the morning. Emily loved to see the drops bouncing on the water.

"It's so soothing to go to sleep when it's raining."

They sat down on the couch, holding hands, their ears perked for Colton's car. They didn't have to talk. Emily put her head on Greg's shoulder. "Don't go to sleep on me." He pulled her up and led her to her bedroom.

Colton came home an hour after Greg left.

The next morning, Emily called Greg. "He came home drunk last night! I've never seen him drunk before. I don't know what's going on with him."

Big Trouble

By the end of January 2002, the board was well aware of how serious the problem was with the lakes. Many samples of lake water had been sent to a laboratory in Pennsylvania—the HOA was fairly sure, but not absolutely certain, that it was golden algae that had caused the fish kill. Among other things, tests indicated that the salt content of the lake water was high. It was well known that salt encourages the golden algae to grow, and as it grows, it consumes more and more of the dissolved oxygen. Eventually, the fish die for lack of oxygen.

Few birds came to the lakes now. Even the turtles looked sick. Most were the non-native red-eared sliders. Their carapaces used to be shiny and black. Now, they were gray and seemed to be peeling. This gave the homeowners something else to stress over. They talked less about dogs off leashes. No one came to the lakes to fish, so that problem was solved. The board could chill out about catching people feeding the ducks because there were none.

Tim, the 'turtle man,' was out of business. He lived on the lower lake and carefully removed exposed turtle eggs from around the lakes, incubated them, and raised the baby turtles in aquariums on the walkway outside his house. He carefully put his aquariums behind bushes so they couldn't be seen from the sidewalk. No one knew for sure, but some suspected that he put the baby turtles back in the lake.

What to do about all of this? Some said, "Don't worry about it. If the lakes are dead, we still have the water to look at." Others said, "The water should be drained off, so we could grow grass at the bottom of the canyon and have two wonderful picnic areas." Others, including the board, thought they may have to remove the water and put clean water in from the city (very expensive!). The lining for the lakes had a life expectancy of only thirty years, and it was thirty-two years ago that Quietwater was developed. So, it would make sense to replace the lining while the lake is drained. To prepare for the worst—draining, replacing the lining, and adding fresh water—the board raised the monthly assessment fee.

"Let's hope 2002 will have a long rainy season." Some other homeowner countered that additional rainwater did not get rid of the salt, nor does evaporation.

Wendy, the board member noted for her optimism, convinced the others to delay the lining decision. "It's just possible that the muck protects the lining." It was decided to send down frogmen to assess the situation. Meanwhile, many plants would be added, and hopefully, they would filter out some of the impurities. The board's plan was to wait and see, keeping fingers crossed.

ANGST

Although Emily never saw Colton drunk again, his glum behavior became acutely troublesome. Ordinarily, he would talk to her and Greg about Russia, the latest developments in its politics, or he would repeat some of the adventures he had had on his last trip. Now, he rarely talked to them at all. There were occasional outbursts like: "Putin is ruthless." When he was asked to elaborate, he said nothing but went to his room and shut the door.

The most she got out of him was when she asked him how Katya was coping with the loss of her husband. He answered: "My God, that woman is brave. I could never do what she does."

"What does she do?"

"You know. What I said in my last lecture!"

He just doesn't want to talk with me, Emily thought. She had Greg to fall back on, but Colton was alone. As far as she could tell, he was spending all his time writing. He only came out of his room to make a cup of tea, which he then took back to his room to drink. He avoided talking to her, not only when Greg was with her in the early evenings, but also when Greg wasn't there. Greg never spent the night when Colton was home. She didn't think Colton was jealous of Greg, or that he thought it was inappropriate for her to have a boyfriend at her age, or that he felt she wasn't respecting the honor of his father.

Emily was so worried that she did something she tried never to do. When he was away at the university one morning, she went into his room to check on what he was working on. Maybe she could figure out what was bothering him. His room was tidy. It had always been neat. Even as a teenager, he put his dirty clothes in the laundry bin. But there were stacks of books everywhere, overflowing the bookcase. Slips of paper as placeholders stuck out of them.

The stacks of paper on the desk seemed to have an order. Emily was struck by the fact that even though he had a large desk (it used to be Ralph's), he had little clear space on top. She recalled being happy that his room had a telephone jack when they first moved here back in 1988. That was before there were cell phones. The telephone was there next to the monitor and the keyboard. He could always take his phone calls in his room, but, now that she thought about it, he rarely got calls. Underneath the desk were the computer tower and a printer. This left little space for his long legs.

The computer was turned off. Next to it was a book—the one he was probably currently reading. A photograph of a woman was being used as a bookmark. Though she looked vaguely familiar, Emily didn't recognize the woman. She looked again… no, she didn't recognize her. Nothing was written on either the front or back of the photo.

Bookends held up other books on his desk: a Russian atlas, a Russian-English dictionary, a book of Russian grammar. There was a small black case. Emily picked it up and realized there was a cell phone inside. Wouldn't he carry his cell phone with him? He had probably forgotten it.

Emily left his room and shut the door, more determined than ever that Colton should move out. He's thirty-nine years old. No matter how glum he is, he needs to be living on his own. She had wanted to tell him so after his last lecture, but he seemed so depressed she didn't have the heart to add to his misery, even though it was obvious that he didn't want to be living with her.

* * *

By March, Emily realized that she couldn't do anything about the golden algae, but she would do her best to bring Colton out of the doldrums. She tried to include him in activities and outings that she and Greg did together. He usually refused to go, and when he did go along with them, he seemed even more miserable. Inevitably, Colton's presence spoiled the experience for all three of them. When Greg's children visited them from the East Coast, he was pleasant but never really enthusiastic. Greg seemed to be running out of patience, and didn't think that the angst Emily felt for her son was doing her much good. Emily knew it was affecting her relationship with Greg.

She considered trying to learn Russian to please Colton, but Emily had no gift for languages, and her age was against her. She caught sight of his grimaces when he heard her attempts at pronunciations. Once she asked him if he would like a dog. He got up and went to his room with no reply.

She even reverted to the direct approach and asked, "Do you know why you are unhappy?" He actually laughed at that question, said "Yes," and went to his room.

Finally, she asked him what he thought about asking Katya to visit them for a couple of weeks. By this time, Emily's probing had ruled out the possibility that Colton was in love with Katya and that she had rejected him. Now, she was back to the idea that Katya was a good friend and someone that he greatly respected. She was almost knocked over by his answer: "Yes, that would be wonderful. I'm not sure she'll feel she should come. She takes her reporting so seriously. On the other hand, she has just published more scathing articles about Putin, so maybe she'd like to get out of the country for a while, for her own safety."

George's Assignment

George came home a half hour later than usual. Lena took one look at him and knew something had happened. He was not his typical calm self. Steve had got up from his chair where he had been reading *Mechanical Engineering* and started to walk out of the room. "Steve come back and sit down, please. I have to tell you both something."

Lena tried to quell her anxiety. We've been caught was her first thought. Fortunately, George was not someone to delay for dramatic purposes, but got right to the point.

"I've been given an assignment."

"Really!" Steve said excitedly. He's probably disappointed, Lena thought, that he hadn't been given one.

"I wish I shared your enthusiasm, Steve." He sat down so he was facing them both. "I have to kill somebody, and, Steve, I'll probably need your help."

"Oh, no," slipped out of Lena's mouth. She immediately realized she had to watch herself. She had plans of her own, which she had kept quiet about. She hoped his assignment wouldn't ruin them.

"Really?" Steve's eyes lit up.

"Fortunately, it's no one we know personally. The woman will be arriving in a couple of weeks. She's Russian, a journalist. So, two weeks is all the time we have to plan how we're going to do it."

As Lena heard the details, she realized it would be an assassination of a Russian national—it would be a personal vendetta of President Putin's. This shows, Lena thought, that

Moscow doesn't value the San Diego sleeper cell. We're only here to do Putin's dirty work. All their training and expertise at spying will be put in jeopardy just to satisfy the ego of one man. She kept these thoughts to herself.

Then she heard George say something that made her heart skip a beat. "….Colton Dunn is her host. He lives in Quietwater with his mother."

George was watching Lena closely. Oh my God! Is he suspicious of me, she wondered? She tried to erase any sign of fear or worry from her face.

"Our job, for now, is to come up with some suggestions as to where and how we can accomplish it."

"This is not our expertise, to say the least. Did they give us any direction?" Lena kept her eyes on George. "Where does this Colton Dunn person live?" she asked. "It's a bit much to kill someone in the very community where we live, don't you think?"

George raised his eyebrows at her last comment, and then added: "I know. I never expected this kind of an assignment," he admitted.

"We'd have to dispose of the body where it could not be found," Lena couldn't help herself. She would never abide performing this deed, but she loved the challenge of analyzing how it should be executed. Besides, she must convince George and Steve that she is emotionally indifferent to the pursuit.

"When do we have to kill her?" Steve asked.

"She flies home Thursday, June 27. They don't want her killed at the airport or any place in public. It would be best if we could just have her disappear. Dunn is an assistant professor at UCSD, but the day before she arrives, he is on summer break, so who knows what he's planning to do."

"Sounds like we should put a camera on the house. We'd have to know what the mother is doing regularly." Lena continued to try to help with their plans, before asking: "Who is the woman visitor?"

"Katya Drozdov, the journalist," George answered.

"Oh yeah, she is covering the Chechen war."

"How do you know that?" Steve asked.

"I go to the library downtown to read the newspapers." Lena wanted to be alone to have time to think. What would she do? Colton is…Oh, Colton…she felt tears coming on. Stop thinking, she told herself. Act tough this minute! Time to be an oak!

"Is there more we should know?" she asked.

George was pensive and shook his head "No."

Lena looked at Steve to try to read his thoughts, but he avoided looking at her. So Lena rose from her chair and said: "Then I'll go start dinner."

She resented Putin for asking them to do this. They, none of them, were trained assassins. Maybe he gave the order in a heated moment and, in a day or two, he'll retract it.

LENA'S PLANS

June 16th came, the day before the journalist was to arrive from Moscow, and Putin still hadn't changed his mind. Lena had been planning to leave the cell for some time. It was a dangerous thing to do because Moscow would search for her relentlessly and kill her, without question. She would never be able to contact George or Steve again. By trying to escape, she would be compromising the cell. The two men would be taken back to Moscow immediately. She knew they would hate that. They both wanted to live the rest of their lives here. She was sorry to have to do this to them, but she felt she had no choice.

She refused to be associated with the impending murder, whoever the victim was, and especially when it was a friend of Colton's. She remembered how highly he spoke about Katya Drozbov. This was the journalist who tried to tell the world the truth about the war in Chechnya. That was another reason she refused to be a part of her death. There was a fourth reason—the most important reason of all: she was pregnant. She was not going to bring up a child in the deceitful situation she was in now.

There was more to it. Once her housemates discovered she was expecting, they would no longer trust her. From every angle, she looked at the problem and she knew she had to try to escape. How to do it was the question she had been asking herself for the last four months. She had a car and felt no guilt about taking the money from her checking account. She would do that on the day she left. She would leave $100 in it, so the account would stay open. Where should she go? That decision easily took her a month. She did her investigating at the library, so no record was on her computer.

In the end, she decided to write Dr. Khassen in Needham, Massachusetts. She did not give a return address. She told the famous Chechen surgeon that she was Chechen, was expecting a baby sometime in September, that she was 42 years old, and had never been married. "The father is a good, wonderful person who has never been married, we love each other but we cannot be together for reasons that I will explain. Would you please let me come to your home and have the baby? I would leave as soon as physically possible, once the baby is born. I realize I am not giving you a way to contact me because I can't do that."

Lena got that far in her plans. The hardest part was when she had to tell Colton she could not see him anymore. She had to protect him and couldn't drag him into her morass any further. She knew he realized that she was a spy. They never talked about it. He was as conflicted as she was. There was no solution that was happy. They would have to give each other up. She told him that both their lives were at stake if they did not. Her pregnancy forced her to reach that difficult decision, but she didn't let him know that she was expecting his child. That would have made it harder for him.

When Lena heard about George's assignment, she knew she had a deadline. She would have to leave just while the men were involved in the murder. At that time, they would have too much on their minds to deal with her disappearance. They might even think she would come back after the murder. She realized that George was suspicious. Although she could get away with wearing baggy clothes because she no longer went to work every day, she caught him looking at her profile. Maybe he would think she had disappeared to get an abortion. That would give her more time to get away.

Katya's Visit

Katya arrived in mid-June, at the beginning of summer vacation for Colton. The timing couldn't be better. It was her first time in the Western Hemisphere. His spirits needed lifting and he wanted to expose her to some of the special features of his country.

They spent two days in San Diego getting reacquainted. His mother insisted on taking both of them on some hikes. Colton's feelings ranged from being amused, embarrassed, and moved. Amused because his mother kept showing off how much she knew about plants, not realizing that Katya would never see another manzanita again. Embarrassed because she made them walk a full mile on a featureless beach just to look at the birds she called skimmers, only the skimmers weren't there. Moved because, in spite of his mother growing old, she kept on trying to achieve things she cared about. He was proud of her.

On the third day, he and Katya took off for the Grand Canyon. Katya was overwhelmed. They had two geology tours, and they spent two nights in one of the lodges. From there, they drove to Los Angeles because Katya definitely wanted to see Universal Studios in Hollywood. She also listed three art museums she wanted to go to, forgetting that each had a considerable entrance fee. In the end, they only went to The Getty. They drove back to San Diego that night so they could sleep at home. They had a day of rest. He showed her Balboa Park.

The next morning, they took off for Mexico, spending the night in Rosarito, where the prices were much more to their liking. Katya was taken by Mexican culture. Rather than go back to San Diego, they decided to park Colton's car at the airport and fly up to San Francisco from Tijuana. Katya said that she would move to San Francisco immediately, if it were at all possible.

"Don't you find the weather too cold?" Colton asked.

"Not at all, this is like the best day of the summer in Odessa. And you say it never freezes here. And it's so interesting, progressive, full of energy."

Colton rented a car so they could drive to Yosemite and Sequoia National Parks. They drove back to San Diego from Tijuana Tuesday night. The next day, Colton had a lengthy meeting at UCSD that he couldn't miss. Emily had to guide a canyoneer hike at the same time.

"Not to worry, I will be enjoying your lovely setting here. I will take a long walk around the Quietwater lakes."

"You should have seen them when we had fish and birds," Emily told her.

"This weather is so pleasant. I love the fragrance of Eucalyptus trees. Their smell is entirely new to me."

When Emily and Colton came back home in the early afternoon on Wednesday, Katya had still not come back to the house. Presumably, she had started her walk later than they expected. The first half hour of waiting they were not worried. After that, Colton decided to go look for her. "Maybe she got lost trying to find her way back to the house." He decided to drive around looking for her. By 5:00 P.M., Emily called Greg and shared her worry.

"Would she have walked to the beach?" Greg asked.

"Golly, that would be far. I know she's used to walking, but she doesn't know how to get around here, and public transportation is so poor. What do you think? Should we call the police?"

"Emily, the police don't respond to a missing person case for 48 hours. She's a mature adult. She knows she can go to someone's home and ask for help. What did she take with her, do you know?"

"Well, that is just it. She didn't take her purse. So her passport and money are all here. She probably doesn't have our telephone number with her. I just hate the thought that she'll be out all night on her own."

"What was she wearing?"

"We were just discussing that. We think she had on darkish-blue slacks and a white shirt or maybe a light blue shirt."

"Isn't she supposed to fly back to Russia tomorrow?"

"Yes."

"Colton has gone around to neighbors asking them to help search for her. She may have fallen down, hit her head and is unconscious somewhere."

"Tell Colton I'll be glad to direct the search, if he would like. I've done this a fair number of times. Even though it is still light out, people should carry a flashlight, in case we need to continue after dark. People should bring their cell phones too, if they have one. I'll be right over."

They searched until midnight. The number of people who helped was gratifying to Emily. Ebony came and George, the chess player. Several others joined in, people Emily didn't know.

A day later, the police were called. Greg spoke to the detective he had trained years ago, Thelma Lee. When she heard that Katya was a Russian national here on a visit, and furthermore, that she was a journalist critical of Putin, she realized she had to inform the FBI field office in San Diego. That meant talking with Special Agent Jake Hughes. Thelma and others in the San Diego police force thought Hughes was a difficult person to work with. He was full of himself and impulsive, but she did her duty and called him.

Thelma had a longtime friend at FBI headquarters in Washington, D.C., Phil Merser, with whom she felt more comfortable. Even though he worked on the opposite side of the country, Thelma had known Phil for over 15 years. She and Phil had gone to the police academy together years ago, and had remained good friends ever since. Phil was a fast talker. The only thing that slowed him down was his need to nibble on something.

He had one of those enviable metabolisms that allowed him to continually eat and never gain weight.

"Yes, it's been on our radar as soon as it was reported in *The San Diego Union Tribune*," Phil told Thelma over the phone. "She could have just wanted to disappear and start a new life."

"We talked about that possibility at this end and decided that was not likely. Evidently, this woman is truly dedicated to reporting what is going on within the present Russian administration. I'm assured by her good friend here that she is not someone who gives up."

Later in the phone conversation, Thelma added: "We were wondering if she has sought asylum but the news hadn't gotten out yet. Would you know?" Thelma heard crunching. It sounded like potato chips. "Evidently, she has had many death threats. She was jailed and tortured on trumped-up charges."

"No, there is nothing in our system that says she has sought asylum." [crunch, crunch]

"Her good friend here, Professor Colton Dunn, doesn't think that's likely anyway. He says that Katya is not someone who thinks about saving her own skin. Evidently, the woman is incredibly brave."

"Sounds like someone Putin would like to terminate," Phil commented.

"That's what Colton thinks."

"If Putin doesn't want to stir up trouble at home, having her mysteriously disappear while she's in another country would be exactly what he would choose to do."

Thelma searched Katya's belongings left in the Dunn home. Neither her cell phone nor her computer suggested that the woman thought she was in danger. Thelma removed some hairs from Katya's hairbrush for a DNA sample and sent them to the lab.

Weeks, then months went by. Colton wrote articles for local newspapers, one for *The Atlantic Monthly*, and one for *Mother Jones* Magazine. He was extensively interviewed by *The New York*

Times. It gave him an avenue to educate the American public about the Chechen war. The 9/11 attack on the World Trade buildings had made the public acutely aware of terrorism, but this case was different. It wasn't an American who had disappeared. Understanding the case required knowing something about current issues in Russia. Concern for Katya spread in other parts of the world, especially in Russia. Many people who didn't appreciate them beforehand began to understand the important role of investigative journalists.

In spite of all the efforts of the San Diego police and the FBI over the next several months, nothing was discovered that shed light on Katya's disappearance. All known leads had been investigated. They had no choice but to declare the Katya Drozdov case open but inactive.

For years, Katya Drozdov had received worldwide acclaim for her dispatches about Chechnya. In Russia, she had the reputation for tenaciously uncovering stories that other reporters refused to touch.

When the Russian public found out about the journalist's disappearance, protests appeared everywhere. Many Russians knew it was not just a disappearance. They knew the woman was dead, somewhere. They knew. The case followed a very familiar pattern. Putin had her killed. The demonstrations accusing Putin of having her murdered went on for weeks. There were gatherings in Grozny and many big cities. In her articles, she had always sympathized with ordinary people whom she saw as caught between rival tyrannies. In Moscow, some citizens created a temporary memorial outside her apartment building to show their respect.

Lena's Trip

On the day Lena left for good, she had two last-minute things to do in the city. She went to the Central Library downtown and sent Colton what appeared to be an official notice from the library, slipping it into the library's mail system. Then she went to her branch bank to withdraw all her money, less $100. Even if George or Steve inquired, the bank would say her account was not closed.

She left her toothbrush, comb, alarm clock, and most of her clothes and books in her room so it wouldn't appear that she had gone for good. Before she stepped into the car, she removed the battery from her burner phone so she couldn't be traced. She drove north on I-15 and turned east on the I-40. She intended to make it to Albuquerque, New Mexico but when she got to Gallup, she couldn't drive any further. She found a motel to spend the night. She was exhausted but she felt the baby kicking. That made her happy. Fortunately, Laika loved riding in the car.

Lena knew that as soon as George and Steve realized that she had actually left home for good, they would have to report it to the handler. That was a given. What she didn't know was if George would pass on his suspicion that she was pregnant. She hoped and hoped that he wouldn't do that, because the handler would want to know who the father was. She didn't think George was aware of Colton.

The next morning, while she paid for her room, she looked at the town map taped to the office countertop. She saw that there was a Walmart on the other side of the railroad tracks that ran through town.

She drove across the tracks and could tell she was in a poorer section of Gallup. The Walmart stood out—the only box store in the region. Breakfast first. She parked at the Jack in the Box next to the Walmart. She had to get rid of her car, in case Moscow had already started looking for her. She had heard that a fast way to get a different car was to swap down, that is, swap a better car for something not as good. As she ate, she sized up the other people in the restaurant. The Walmart parking lot was beginning to fill up, but Lena thought she'd have better luck approaching someone who was seated, relaxed, and eating breakfast.

She approached a Navaho couple and asked: "Do you know someone who would like to swap their car for a 2000 year Ford Focus?" The Navaho man looked at his wife. Lena thought maybe they hadn't understood what she said. Should she say it again? She didn't want to appear impatient.

The woman turned to the man, probably her husband, and said, "We should send her to John Pete's."

He thought about it, then finally said: "Ya, it's 10 miles northwest of here on Hwy 53. It's not on the reservation, not that far away, but it's a good Navajo trading post. John Pete Cloud has his used car dealership there." The man sounded like he thought Lena lived in the area.

"He's my husband's brother," the woman explained. "He should give you a good deal."

"If you can wait for us, we just have to drop something off, then we'll be ready to go back home. We can show you right where to go."

Lena agreed. It was her first conversation with American Indians. The simplicity and directness of their speech was refreshing. A half-hour later she was following their Chevy pickup. She figured it had been new sometime around 1990. Once on the 53, the road became bumpy and ill-repaired. It wasn't a highway but a third-rate county road.

John Pete's turned out to be a small dealership, indeed! No more than 20 cars and trucks were in the lot. She talked for some time to John Pete Cloud, and her instinct told her that he was truthful. This leap of faith was so unlike her. Probably the only person she had ever trusted before was Colton. For once, she wished Steve were with her. As objectionable of a person as he was, he did know mechanical stuff.

She traded her 2000 Ford Focus for a 1995 Chevy Impala. She could see that the Chevy needed two new tires, but it seemed to run smoothly.

She asked John Pete not to process the papers for five days as she needed a head start to get away from her husband who was after her. She explained that he was an abusive man with a violent streak. She had to leave him. She had to lie. She was good at lying, even an accomplished liar, you might say, but she longed for a day when she wouldn't have to lie anymore.

In Albuquerque, Lena drove her Impala to a Chevy dealer to have the car looked over. She bought two new tires. From Albuquerque, she and Laika continued their journey, taking the I-40 to Oklahoma City. The following day they made it to St. Louis on the 44. She slept an extra couple of hours in the motel. On the fourth day, she drove to Columbus, Ohio on the I-70. From there, she headed north to pick up the Pennsylvania Turnpike. That was just about as far as her planning took her. Once she got to New York, she would rely on advice from others.

Driving for hours each day gave her much time to think. She felt guilty abandoning George and Steve, but, on the other hand, she would never be able to get a job in San Diego (or probably anywhere) under the name of Lena Hansen. She had to go elsewhere and change her identity, if she were ever going to work again. If she had stayed in the Toyon house and had the baby, she would have been afraid of Steve losing his temper with the first smelly diaper, the first night he was kept awake.

Of course, she thought of Colton all the time. To have to be cruel to someone she loved had been the hardest thing she had ever had to do. He wasn't just someone she loved. He was a friend, the only friend she had ever had. It would make her deliriously happy if she could just share with him that they were having a baby. He probably thinks that everything I said to him was just fabricated to fulfill some selfish goal. He needed her too. Together they were complete.

Moscow would never let her disappear. They would always come after her. Colton wouldn't be safe. The baby wouldn't be safe.

She was hungry again, always glad for an excuse to stop. The Pennsylvania Turnpike had good service plazas. She was careful to eat only healthy food and not a lot at any one time. That helped to keep her awake. She had a rule that she wouldn't nibble on snacks or drink in the car. Frequent stops were good. Lena loved walking Laika. Usually, there was an area away from cars where it was safe to let her off the leash so she could run around.

Once back in the car, she turned the radio on to keep her company. However, from the Rockies through the Midwest, the selection of programs was poor. Most stations reported news with a decidedly conservative bent. The music was not to her liking either. The classical channels were crackly beyond enjoyment. Evangelical preaching was at every turn of the dial. Once on the Pennsylvania Turnpike, however, the quality started to improve. Her Chevy Impala had a tape deck, but Lena had no tapes. She had never caught on to playing them.

She couldn't decide if she should send Dr. Khassen a letter saying that she was about to arrive. Since she still couldn't use her phone for fear of being tracked, she decided not to let him know in advance. It would seem presumptuous on her part if she did contact him and gave him no way to contact her. She arrived at Needham on the sixth day and decided to spend the night in a motel outside of town, so she could be fully rested when she got to his house. But as tired as she was from six days straight of driving, she didn't sleep well that night. What would she do if he refused to help her? What if he wasn't home? What if he no longer lived there? What if he was no longer alive?

Lena parked in front of 301 Maple Street at 10:00 in the morning. She rang the doorbell, holding Laika on a leash. What an unusual doorbell chime: Beethoven's Fifth. A gray-haired woman answered: "Hello." Her eyes settled on Lena's stomach. Lena introduced herself, but wasn't sure the woman was paying attention, as she simultaneously smiled, teared up, and yelled "Baiev," over her shoulder. Then she must have remembered her manners, for she grabbed Lena's hand and led her inside. "Baiev, she's here!"

MISSION TRAILS PARK

Two years later, on May 8, 2004, a hiker dialed 911: "I believe," he took in a deep breath, "I know, there is a body buried here."

"What's your name and where are you?"

"I'm Louis Jeffery." He had to take in more air. "I'm...I'm in Mission Trails Park. The shoe is sticking out of the ground but I see..."

"Mr. Jeffery, it is most important that you don't touch a thing. Please stand away from the body. Now where are you in Mission Trails Park?"

"I'm in the West Sycamore part. I was..."

"Are you alone?"

"Yes."

"Are you in sight of any road or landmark?"

"I took the trailhead off of Stonebridge Parkway. There's a gate there..."

"OK, that puts you in San Diego City. Wait there please. How far along that trail did you get? "

"About a third of a mile, I think. Oh, I should have said I left the trail to walk down toward the streambed. The stream has no water in it..."

An hour later, Homicide Detective Sergeant Thelma Lee and Detective Jim Shaw arrived at the crime scene in Mission Trails Park. By then, several patrol officers were there. They were the first responders. The crime scene had been taped off. The witness, Louis Jeffery, a pale kid, no more than 19 years old, sat quietly on the bank nearby. He had already been interviewed by a patrol officer.

The crime scene analyst had taken the necessary photos for the police. Doug Cooper, a reporter from *The San Diego Union Tribune*, was taking photos of the corpse and Mr. Jeffery. By knowing the radio frequency that the police use, local media can monitor police calls and respond quickly to any incident that sounds newsworthy.

Once the other detectives on Thelma Lee's team had arrived, the patrol sergeant gathered everyone together so he could brief them on the facts. Detective Shaw took down all the pertinent information on his notepad. When the briefing was over, Detective Lee thanked the patrol sergeant, who then drove off with most of the other patrol officers, leaving two behind to help guard the crime scene.

Now, Detective Sergeant Lee was free to lead her own investigation. She started inspecting the corpse, and took her own photographs, knowing they would not be as good as those taken by the crime scene analyst, but she knew that it never hurt to have more photos. She thought back to the Svenson murder, when those photos somehow disappeared. What a nightmare case that was to solve! Ever since, she had always snapped a few photos of her own.

Thelma had no doubts that the victim was murdered. Why else would a body be put off the trail, out of sight, and with no marker? No grave was dug. Lack of time, or was the murderer confident that the corpse would not be found? The body had been covered with about three inches of soil, no more. The less soil coverage, the faster a corpse decays. Murderers usually want that process to be fast, making the remains harder to identify when they are found. The trade-off is that too little soil coverage might make the corpse detectable by vultures. Not that the murderer cared if the cadaver was eaten by birds or other critters, but park rangers will investigate an area under circling vultures.

Louis Jeffery, the hiker, had called 911 saying that he spotted a sneaker sticking out of the ground and that was what got his attention. But Thelma smelled urine and saw that the gym shoe was damp and free of dirt. Poor kid, he must have been so scared when he realized he was peeing on the foot of a corpse.

Thelma and Jim searched the area for footprints. They asked Louis, the hiker, to remove his boots. More photographs. Thelma introduced herself and asked him to please repeat how he had found the body.

Jim had recorded the hiker's account of discovering the body. The young man didn't seem to mind repeating his story. He continued to wait patiently out of the way. Thelma read Jim's notes and noticed there was no mention of the peeing incident. Nonetheless, Thelma was grateful for the witness's cooperation and apparent emotional stability. Jim was now free to help Thelma with another task.

With the same care as an archeologist, the crime scene photographer had brushed away the soil on top of the skeleton enabling Thelma to clearly see the shape and position of the deceased. Jim was ready to take notes again. The two of them, Jim and Thelma, had performed this routine several times before.

"The corpse is in the skeletonizing stage of decomposition," Thelma called out. That was perfectly obvious, of course, but she had been trained to never overlook recording the obvious. Sometimes, if a corpse was constantly exposed to hot sunlight, the last of the soft parts would mummify. She had Jim take note of the environment. The numerous trees in this area had kept the corpse in the shade.

Thelma proceeded to make some guesstimates, knowing full well that the medical examiner's findings would be much more reliable. This procedure sharpened her observation skills while giving her some basic facts she could immediately work with. "I would say this person has been decomposing for about two years." To determine the gender, Thelma had to kneel on the ground close to the corpse. "Female certainly, judging from the width and shallowness of the pelvis." Thelma didn't bother taking actual measurements. The medical examiner would do that later.

She next inspected the skull. "The victim's hair has fallen out.

A good amount of hair at that! We should have no trouble getting a decent DNA sample." Thelma moved nearer to the head and bent over close so she could inspect the suture lines on the scull. Thank goodness it was in the middle of the day, she thought. You need good light to see the suture lines, especially when they are fused as those of this woman. "The suture lines—all three of the major ones—appear fused, so she was older than 50 when she died."

Thelma recalled working with the former Detective Sergeant, Greg McDonald. Over the years, she and Greg had become friends. She was grateful for all that he had taught her. Thelma had been one of the first woman detectives in the SDPD. Her success was, in part, due to Greg, who didn't feel threatened by having a female partner. She knew she had some rough edges. His example helped her to become more humble. She still felt superior to several of the other detectives, but Greg had trained her not to let such an attitude show.

Another personal characteristic that could get her into trouble was her confidence. It could lead her down investigative paths she was told (sometimes ordered) never to go. Over their years together, Greg had had to reel her in several times.

Now he's retired and living in that boring development. What was it called…Quietwater? That name says it all! She really should pay him a visit. The last time she saw Greg was when Katya Drozdov disappeared. Oh my God! This corpse might be that missing journalist.

The last estimate Thelma had to make was the woman's height. She took out her flashlight, which she knew to be eight inches long. Someone's height was roughly four times the length of their femur. Hum, her femur is almost two flashlights long. That's 16 inches. So the woman was 5'4" tall.

"To summarize:" she said, looking at Jim, "the victim was a woman over fifty, 5'4" tall. There is no apparent sign of the cause of her death. Her body was discarded in a remote area, minimally buried, about two years ago."

Scuba Divers

It was a lovely, balmy evening in May. Greg and Emily were seated on Emily's deck, occasionally holding hands while they chatted. Although it was past nine o'clock, the reflection from the gibbous moon gave them enough light to see each other while they sipped on their glasses of wine. Greg had just finished telling Emily about the call he had received from Thelma Lee. He had to remind Emily that Thelma was the detective from the SDPD who handled the Katya Drozdov case.

"Oh yes, I remember."

Greg went on to tell Emily about the corpse found in Mission Trails Park and that it could be the remains of Katya. He let that settle in Emily's thoughts.

"Is it possible?" Emily said. "It's such a dreadful thought. That powerful woman now is nothing more than a heap of bones."

"It will happen to us all."

"Part of me wants it to be Katya, so her disappearance would be solved, but of course, I would much rather that she were still alive somewhere. Should we tell Colton?"

"I think we can be sure that Katya is dead, even if that isn't her skeleton. Let's wait a few days before telling Colton. Thelma said there was plenty of hair for a good DNA analysis. Remember, two years ago, Thelma ran a DNA analysis on the hair in Katya's hairbrush?"

"Yes."

"The test should tell if it matches that of Katya."

"Yes, it's wise to not tell Colton until we know for sure. No sense getting him all worked up again. Especially since the last several months he has seemed back to his normal self, don't you think?"

"Yes, I guess so, but I don't see him much…. There wasn't a lot left of the woman's personal effects, only the trainers, patches of blue material of some sort."

Emily wanted to change the subject: "Well, tell me: when are the frogmen scheduled to come?"

"Next Thursday, although I do think the lake is looking better. It's clearing up, don't you think?"

"Yes, everybody I've spoken to says it looks better."

"God knows why…."

"How did you get the frogmen?"

"We should really call them scuba divers. They do alot of work with the police. They are trained in rescue and underwater forensic matters. It costs a hell of a lot of money, but without draining the lakes, we have no other means of judging the condition of the lining. It's delicate work, because we don't want any probing to harm it."

* * *

The following Thursday morning, Emily and Greg were sitting out on Greg's deck. It didn't have as nice a view as that from Emily's. Greg had cooked an eggs-and-bacon breakfast for the two of them. It was so pleasant to be with him, she thought. She didn't worry about Colton. He made his own bowl of cereal every morning.

What is wrong with him? She asked herself. The man's 41 years old. He doesn't need her. This time she really meant it. If he didn't move out by the end of this year, she decided, she'd ask him to leave, for his own good. He makes plenty of money. He can afford a place on his own. She wasn't even sure he enjoyed living in Quietwater. He never walks around the lakes. He rarely sits out on the deck.

* * *

By 10:00 A.M. that same morning, several homeowners, including Greg and Emily, had congregated down at the upper lake to watch the scuba divers. Fortunately, the day was overcast, or 'May gray' as they say in San Diego, making it comfortable for the spectators to stand around waiting.

"We don't know exactly how deep the lakes are or what shape the lakes' floors are," Greg admitted to Emily and the others standing around. He had tried to do his homework. He knew both the length of time a diver spends underwater and at what depth determines if decompression measures need to be taken. The internet said decompression measures are necessary if a diver spends more than about 4 hours in 30 feet of water. But Greg guessed the upper lake was about 16 feet deep. So no problem with that was anticipated.

The two divers, with scuba tanks on their backs, started at the upper lake, the larger of the two. They crisscrossed the width, back and forth, until they met in the middle. Seventy minutes later, they came out of the water, took off their gear, and reported their findings.

"All looks fine," one said. "The deepest it got was 18 feet, I would say. What did you think, Weston?"

"About the same. The slope down to the deepest part is gradual. No sign of damage to the lining that I could see." Weston looked at Tom for his opinion.

"I saw no damage. There's about a foot of muck at that deepest part, and less where it's shallow." Weston had retrieved a pink high heel, and Tom a red plastic bucket, the size a child would use.

The bystanders were relieved. Jokes went around, of course, about the pink high heel.

Greg thanked the men and said, "Did you happen to see any fish down there?"

"Yeah, I saw a couple of trout."

"Good heavens, we thought they had all died!" The other diver confirmed that he had seen a couple, too.

"That's interesting…. Do you want to relax a bit, perhaps have your lunch, and then, whenever you're ready, you can tackle the lower lake? It's smaller."

The divers' report about the lower lake was much the same. It was not as deep, but its slopes were steeper and the muck about as thick. However, Tom came up first and handed a dog collar to Greg. "I wouldn't have noticed this, but the tag on the collar was bright." His voice was muffled because he hadn't removed his headgear. "I've got to go back in and help Weston with the drones."

"Drones?"

"Drones!"

In no time, people were on their phones, dialing neighbors.

As Tom went back in the water, Weston emerged with the first drone, put it on the path, and went back into the lake. Eventually three drones were brought out.

"Oh, how I wish Ebony were here." Emily walked quickly back home to call her. While she was at it, she'd tell Colton. Knocking on his door, Emily called out: "Colton, guess what they found in the lake." When his door opened he looked paler than usual.

"What? What did they find?"

"Three drones, a pink high heel, oh, and a dog collar."

"A dog collar? Which lake?"

"The lower one. I'm going to call Ebony." She was prepared to coax him to go down there with her so he could have a look, but as she picked up the phone, she realized that he had already left the house. Back down at the lake, Emily saw Colton was holding the dog collar in his hand.

Ebony showed up and shouted: "Vindicated, at last!" Emily laughed with her. They both inspected the drones. "They look homemade," Ebony said.

Greg and another board member discussed the fee that the scuba divers requested. They asked them to put their findings in a report for the HOA's records. Once free, Emily said to both Greg and Ebony: "Let's celebrate. Why don't you both come over to dinner tonight?"

"We do have good reason to celebrate," Greg said. "The lake linings seem OK, and you two are no longer considered kooks.

The UFOs are actually drones." Emily felt her face blushing.

"Don't worry, Emily. I already knew people called me UFO. Yes, let's celebrate."

That night, the three of them were on the deck chatting before dinner.

"I'd love to meet your son, Emily. Is he going to have dinner with us? I didn't get a chance to meet him down at the lake."

"I hope so. I have to do one last thing in the kitchen and then I'll call him."

"I'll get him," Greg said, not looking at Emily for approval. He got up, went downstairs, and knocked on Colton's door. "Hey Colt, we need you upstairs. Emily is about to serve up dinner." No answer. Greg asked, "Are you all right? I'm coming in."

Colton was sitting at his desk. He had been crying. Greg noticed the dog collar lying on the desk in front of him. "Do you know something about that dog collar?"

"I'm sorry I've been difficult, I'll come up right away. I'm just going to wash my face."

Over dinner, Ebony said there was another upcoming get-together with some of the astronomers that had fancy telescopes. "This time they plan to have it close by, on Mount Fortuna in Mission Trails Park."

"Oh, I'd love to go." Emily was feeling a little giddy from the wine and all the excitement over what had happened in the last day or two. Without thinking she blurted out, "That reminds me. How's the murder investigation going, Greg?" She turned toward Ebony to say, "A body was found in Mission Trails Park."

Greg hesitated and tried to give Emily a discouraging look. "Well, I'm not sure how the investigation is going. I'm retired from that kind of work."

"Really," Ebony perked up and asked, "What kind of a policeman were you?"

"I was a homicide detective."

"That's why a friend of his in the police department consulted with Greg about this murder. Thelma Lee is her name," Emily added. "She doesn't think Greg has anything to do in his retirement."

"That certainly is not true. My goodness, no! Well, do you know who the victim was?" Ebony asked.

"No." Greg wished the subject would change.

"Was it a man or a woman?"

"It was a woman around 50 years old." Immediately, Greg realized he shouldn't have divulged that information in front of Colton.

"When was she killed?" Colton asked.

Too late, Greg thought. He'll put two and two together. "They think about two years ago."

"Do you know how tall she was?"

Greg hesitated before answering, seeing that Colton was getting emotional. "Yes, about 5 foot 4 inches tall."

Colton put his head in his hands. Emily and Greg exchanged glances. She put her hand on his shoulder, "What's wrong, Colton?"

"I hope I'm wrong. We can talk about it later."

Everybody was quiet. Emily served the sherbet. A few comments were made about how grateful they were for the evening's breeze. Ebony got the hint and left right after dessert. Normally, Colton would have gone straight to his room, but as soon as the door shut behind Ebony, he turned to Greg and asked: "What else do you know about the woman. Was she murdered?"

"It appears so. The police can get her DNA." By this time, Greg could tell Emily realized what she had done. Although it was too late, she remained quiet.

"I knew a woman. Her name was Lena. She disappeared two years ago. She was scared. I wonder if she is the victim."

Both Emily and Greg were surprised. "You don't mean Katya?" Emily asked.

"No....Oh, I see what you mean. The woman could be Katya," Colton replied.

They all were quiet until Greg asked him to tell them about

the other woman. "Lena, you say?"

"Yes, I never knew her last name or where she lived."

This is very peculiar, Greg was thinking. "Not Lena Hansen?" Colton made no reply. "Did she live in Quietwater?" When Colton again did not reply, Greg turned toward Emily and explained to her that Lena Hansen was George Hansen's wife.

Colton looked down and was quiet. Emily started to clear the table.

Finally, Colton said something. "I don't know whose wife she was. I never knew where she lived as I said. I didn't know if she was married or not."

"Did she have a dog?" Greg asked.

"Yes, little Laika." With that he ran down the stairs and reappeared with the dog collar, which he showed to his mother and Greg.

"Oh my, it says 'Laika,'" said Greg, passing the dog collar on to Emily so she could read the name on it.

"I know she was Russian, but she claimed to be American."

Greg was trying to make sense of what Colton said. "Emily and I were thinking the dead woman found in Mission Trails Park might be Katya, but now you are suggesting she could be this woman, Lena?"

"Well, maybe, something's going on around here."

"I have to bring Thelma Lee into this. She is an excellent detective. She's the one who has authority. I have none. I'll call her now. Maybe she can come over first thing in the morning to talk with you."

"I have a class to teach tomorrow morning at 10:00."

After being briefed by Greg over the phone, Thelma and Detective Shaw came right over. "Best to act quickly before word gets around in the community," she said. Colton handed her the dog collar. She looked at it on both sides. "What's this here? It feels like a piece of Velco."

Colton didn't know. Thelma asked him how he had met Lena, what was she like, etc.

"We used to read books and talk about them. She was very bright and had a wonderful sense of humor."

Poor dear, Emily thought, it seems like he was in love with this Lena. That might help explain his behavior the last few years.

Thelma took over the conversation: "OK, we have: ①A dead woman killed approximately two years ago whose DNA we are determining. ②The DNA of a woman, Katya, who went missing two years ago. (Many people believe, without proof, that Putin contracted her disappearance and death.) ③Another woman, Lena, possibly Russian, who had a dog named Laika, also went missing two years ago. ④Laika's dog collar found in the lake. ⑤Three handmade drones found in the lake.

"Colton, do you have anything that could be used to get Lena's DNA?" Thelma asked.

After showing Thelma a photo of Lena and some books that he knew Lena had read, she told him: "I have no idea if these will be sufficient for a good DNA sample. The lab will tell us." She paused to think for a moment before saying to Greg: "I think the first thing is to have you pay a friendly visit to the Hansen's and ask to speak with Lena. Can you think of an excuse without mentioning the dog collar that was found in the lake?"

"Yes, sure," he answered, but then it occurred to him that he had better relay to Thelma his run-in with Steve Hansen several years ago.

"Hmm, could he have been making drones in the garage?" Thelma asked.

"I suppose that's possible, but why the secrecy?" Greg asked Thelma.

"Interesting," she replied, "two Russian women, both missing."

Greg wondered if Lena had simply wanted to stay away from Colton for the last two years. Why would Colton not know where she lived? Maybe she just didn't want to see him again. In that case, Lena could still be living at 2961 Toyon Drive.

Later that night, Greg thought again about how Colton suspected that Lena was the dead woman in the park, not Katya.

Maybe, in his mind, he had already given up on Katya being alive. He had known for a long time that she was probably dead. But he didn't know about Lena. Was he really worried that Lena may have been murdered? Did he have any other reason to suspect that she had been murdered, other than he knew she was scared?

Since Greg had never met Lena, Emily volunteered to be the one to go to the Hansen house.

"I think I met her years ago." Emily said, recalling the word-of-the-day discussion. It all came back to her about the plant that she had been interested in. "I could take her a gift of a Heavenly Bamboo plant. If she is there, I'll recognize her for sure, now that I've seen Colton's photo. Even if she's suspicious as to why, after nine years, I would be thinking of her to bring her a gift, I'll be able to find out if she's living there."

"You'll have to do it when they are home from work. I'll be keeping a lookout on the house from four o'clock on, and call you when I know they're home."

* * *

After hearing from Greg, Emily drove to the Toyon address with a small Heavenly Bamboo plant in the passenger footwell. She decided to leave it there until she knew that Lena would come to the door. She couldn't find the doorbell so she knocked. Her knock was pathetic, so she knocked again. Her knuckles hurt. Finally the door opened. A young man hung on to the door while uttering an unenthusiastic: "Hello?"

"Hello, may I speak to Lena, please," Emily said with a friendly smile. She realized the man must be Steve.

"She's not here."

"Do you know when she'll be home?"

He turned around and shouted into the house: "Dad." He waited. "Dad, a woman's here who wants to see Mom." George appeared around the corner.

"Oh, hello. I recognize you. You're Greg's friend, aren't you?"

"Yes, that's right. I know Greg enjoys playing chess with you. Nice to see you. George, is it?"

"Yes, well, I'm sorry to disappoint you, but Lena's not here."

Emily tried to look disappointed. "Do you know when she'll be back?"

"I wish I knew the answer to that question. I don't think she's coming back."

"Oh, really? Should I come back tomorrow?"

"She left us a couple of years ago."

"Oh, my goodness, I had no idea. Oh, I am sorry. I brought her a plant. I should have brought it to her years ago. I'm so sorry for your loss." Emily paused not knowing what to say. "That must have been difficult for both you and your son."

George closed his eyes and grimaced, while nodding 'yes' with his head.

"Where did she move to?" Emily continued.

"We have no idea. We haven't heard from her since. I wish we could help you."

"I don't think Greg knows."

"I'm sure he doesn't, otherwise you wouldn't be here, but thank you for thinking of her." There was something about George's expression that made Emily think that he doubted her sincerity.

* * *

Two nights later, Thelma and Jim returned to the Dunn home to ask Colton more questions. Thelma started the interview by summarizing what they already knew about Lena. "OK, we now know that Lena is either forcibly missing, 'disappeared' as they say in Mexico, or willfully missing, and perhaps in hiding, or she may be dead."

Colton sat there with his eyes downcast.

"From Lena Hansen's 1040 filing, her former employer was General Atomics. GA is a San Diego firm, which, among other things, makes equipment bought by the U.S. military. Since we learned about the drones found in the lake, I inquired if General Atomics is developing drones. The answer is yes."

"Really?"

"This is beginning to look interesting, isn't it?" Thelma said. "I believe you told us that Lena had lost her job. Is that correct?"

"Yes. The last six months that we were seeing each other she was not working."

"How and where did you see each other?" Thelma asked.

"At the library. We'd do that during the day when the people she lived with were at work."

"What kind of car did she drive?"

"I'm afraid I don't know."

"Did she take Laika with her to the library?"

"No. She left her at home."

When Thelma finished her questioning, she thanked him and left the Dunn home, relieved that he hadn't inquired about the results of the DNA test of the skeleton in Mission Trails Park, which she had been ordered not to reveal.

* * *

The next morning, Thelma and Jim went to the personnel office of General Atomics. They approached the desk of the receptionist and presented her their cards. "I am Homicide Detective Sergeant Lee of the San Diego Police Department. This is Detective Shaw."

The receptionist looked at Thelma's card closely, then said: "Thelma Lee, where in the south are you from?"

Thelma looked at the nameplate on the receptionist's desk before answering her directly: "I was born in southern Virginia, Susan, but I lived mostly in Massachusetts growing up. Are you from the South?"

"No, I've lived in San Diego my entire life; boring!"

"Well, it's a good boring—we're lucky to live here." Thelma forced herself to give a little laugh. This is the kind of thing she hated to do—small talk. Greg had taught her that small talk is important. "I'm here to inquire about a former General Atomics employee whose name is Lena Hansen. Could I speak with your head of personnel?"

"Do you have an appointment?"

Thelma stared intently at her and said, "No. It concerns a murder investigation."

Susan's eyes opened up wide. "I see," she said picking up the telephone. "Mrs. Verdin, excuse me for interrupting you, there are two policemen, ah, officers out here wanting to speak with you…about a former employee."

There was a pause, then Susan asked Thelma: "What did you say the name of the employee was?"

"Lena Hansen."

The receptionist repeated the name into the phone. "I see; yes, ma'am. I see…yes, ma'am." Susan hung up and offered them some coffee while they waited.

In a couple of minutes, Mrs. Verdin came out, introduced herself, and directed Thelma and Jim to her office. Before she shut the door, she turned around to address Susan: "As soon as Mr. Carmichael comes, please send him in."

Thelma noted Mrs. Verdin was quite nervous, and pretended to be searching her files for information about Lena Hansen. A few minutes later, Mr. Carmichael came in. After hellos and introductions, Mr. Carmichael turned to Mrs. Verdin and said: "OK, Dorothy, I can take it from here. Thank you."

Thelma had studied what the internet told her about General Atomics. She knew that Fred Carmichael was the vice president and controller. He sat down at Mrs. Verdin's desk and opened up a file which he had brought with him. Thelma saw that he quickly disconnected the phone. He wanted to be sure no one interrupts or listens in, Thelma thought.

"Yes, well now, you want to know about Lena Hansen, I've heard. What exactly did you want to know?"

Thelma gave him the same stare she had given Susan. In fact, down at the station, Thelma was known for her steely-eyed stares. They called her SE for short. The look was guaranteed to make any human target squirm.

Mr. Carmichael looked down at the file. "Let's see, she was hired on March 9, 1989, and we let her go on September 3, 2001."

He looked up from the file, then back down and rustled through a few pages. "She was what we call a 'computer program cleanser.' She took out the bugs and made programs run more smoothly. What else would you like to know?"

"Who was her immediate boss? What types of programs did she clean? And why did GA fire her?" That last question was what Thelma really wanted the answer to, but Mr. Carmichael avoided it.

Thelma knew she was getting the runaround. "How many promotions was she given?" Mr. Carmichael hesitated, rustling through pages again to delay, or pretend he couldn't find the answer. Thelma answered for him: "I believe it was a minimum of three." She had inquired earlier of the crime analysis unit to find out about Lena's work record. "Mr. Carmichael, this is not just a casual interest on our part. You and your company are being questioned in regards to a murder investigation. If you avoid answering my questions, or if we don't think you are answering the question honestly, we will have to pursue other means of getting the information. This will be done publicly. You have the opportunity now to answer us informally, and you may save yourself some embarrassment."

A look of resignation came onto his face. "OK, message received. Evidently, Lena Hansen was much smarter than her boss and others gave her credit for. We eventually discovered that she had stolen the login code off of her boss's computer and was harvesting information from it. She probably had been doing it for several years."

"So, you suspect industrial espionage? My next question is: 'Who was her benefactor?'"

"We don't know, but we have her last theft on camera, absolute proof…. No, we have no idea who she was working for."

"Why didn't you bring in the police?"

"Our products are sold to the military. We could lose contracts if they think we are not secure. I'm telling you, this woman was a real professional. We were careful." Mr. Carmichael, then went through all the security measures the company had taken.

"We would like to see the tapes."

"Yes, we can do that. We would greatly appreciate it if this doesn't get out." Mr. Carmichael picked up the phone: "Jason, please set up the film with LH in my office. I'll be there in a minute with the police. Make sure no one else goes in." He hung up and stood, collecting the papers in the file he had brought with him. "You know about that damn dog, Laika, I think she called it?"

"No. I mean I know she had a dog named Laika, but what else is there to know about the dog?"

"Let's wait until we get to my office and I'll show you."

SDPD

Back at the station, Thelma went into her office and shut the door. There was a plethora of information to think about. It seemed that she had two cases: one a homicide and another industrial espionage. The two were not necessarily related. Should she turn the espionage case over to her friend, Phil, in the FBI? Maybe not yet. She was having fun with the possibility that the two cases might be connected.

She reviewed in her mind the film she was shown in Mr. Carmichael's office. The woman, Lena, was somewhat attractive: dark wavy hair with pleasant features was all she could tell from the video. Was Colton drawn to her romantically or just intellectually? Would Lena be attracted to him or was she just playing with him? Russia seemed to be what drew them together.

Although Thelma went home from work, she couldn't keep from thinking about the case. While making a stir-fry for her dinner, she asked herself: Why wouldn't Lena tell Colton where she lived or her last name?

Thelma started washing the dinner dishes. She says she's American. But Colton knows she's Russian.

A semi-desert, San Diego was always close to drought conditions. So, as not to waste water, Thelma started mopping her kitchen floor with the leftover dishwater. Oh my God, it's staring me right in the face! She's a Russian spy. How could I have missed it? Does Colton know? Oh, poor guy!

Greg had told her that the Hansen family was strange. The son doesn't look like either parent. No wonder. They're slick, trained by the best. Maybe there's a Russian cell operating out of Quietwater. Who would believe that? It's so obvious, it's embarrassing!

Now, it's definitely the time to call Phil. Darn, I'll have to wait for morning. Phil worked at the FBI's headquarters in D.C. She looked up his number so she could call him first thing in the morning. In fact, she'd get up at six so she could reach him at his office at 9:00 A.M.

Laika…the space mutt…right in our damn faces!

* * *

"Gees, Thelma, you have a knack for calling me at the worst time!" Phil was quietly chuckling.

"Sorry, did I interrupt your second breakfast?"

"Worse, my vacation was due to start tomorrow, and now I've been assigned this Drozdov case."

"Well, I may be able to help you with that. Listen to my news."

"OK, I'm all ears. Shoot!"

Thelma heard crunching over the phone as she explained the case from the beginning. Halfway through, Phil interrupted her: "Wait, this is sounding like it's connected to the Katya Drozdov case."

"Yes, but I'm not sure exactly how. But, Phil, let me finish…."

After telling him about Lena Hansen, Colton, Laika, etc., Phil's immediate reply was: "OK, very interesting. What are all the Hansen names—their American names, that is?"

"George Hansen, Lena Hansen, and Steve Hansen," Thelma told him. She was trying not to get impatient.

As he often did, Phil suddenly changed the subject, saying, "You know, we haven't actually seen you in person since Linda and I went camping with you and your cyclist friend, what was his name?"

"Michael Ball."

"That was a great trip we all had together. I'm not trying to change the subject, but Linda won't forgive me if I don't ask you if anything came of that relationship?"

"Nothing came of it. Now back to the point:…"

Phil finally concentrated and summarized: "OK, you want me

to find out the Russian names of the three Hansens. That's fine. I have to do that for my own investigation, and since we're working on the same case, I guess I'll be able to share that information with you. Best if your captain grants you a temporary duty assignment, so you can officially work with us."

Thelma answered: "Perhaps later; I'm just getting started on the case here at this end. If they ever granted me a temporary assignment, it would only be for a week."

"Well, don't hold your breath," Phil said. "This type of info could take weeks to uncover. Send me all that you have. Now, I have to go home and tell Linda our vacation will be put off a month."

"Thanks, Phil. I'll FedEx everything I have. Give my best to Linda."

Thelma wanted to ask Phil why the FBI had ordered the SDPD not to release the DNA results of the Mission Trails corpse. A few weeks ago, her police lab had confirmed that the DNA profile matched that of Katya Drozdov. Thelma wanted to know why the finding could not be made public. Did the FBI already suspect the Hansen men of the murder and not want them to do a runner if the body of Katya Drozdov was identified?

She was sure that there was a connection between the two disappearing Russian women, both in the vicinity of Quietwater. But, she also knew she would just have to accept it: the FBI didn't have to disclose its reasons. At least Phil will be willing to give her the Hansens' Russian names, once he finds out what they are.

* * *

Over the next couple of weeks, nothing much was accomplished on either case. The lab had difficulties getting Lena's DNA profile from the material Colton had turned over. Thelma would have loved to search the Hansen house, but that was impossible.

Three weeks after talking to Phil, Thelma's captain told her that the local FBI office had requested (ordered!) SDPD to drop its activity on the Hansen case. Evidently, local FBI agents (headed by Special Agent Jake Hughes) were planning to raid the Hansen house. "What are they going to do, arrest them for illegal entry to the States using forged documents?" Thelma asked.

The very next day, Phil called her to give her the Hansens' Russian names. That was relatively quick, she thought. Phil told her that he had consulted with a CIA agent who, in turn, had solicited the help of a U.S. operative in Moscow to find the Russian names. George, Steve, and Lena Hansen were really: Grigory Dudko, Stanislav Yegorov, and Lena Yurin, respectively.

The CIA must also be investigating the case, Thelma thought. She probably won't be able to get any more information from Phil from now on. Thelma asked Phil about the Hansen home raid. He laughed, "No. That was such a jackass idea it was immediately called off. Everyone is now in agreement that the Hansens are more valuable for what they can lead us to—other Russian agents, especially their handler."

That afternoon, the captain winked at Thelma, knowing she was pleased when he told her: "You're on the case again, good luck! Oh, I should tell you that all those local FBI guys have done so far is to put up cameras outside the Hansen residence."

Thelma was excited to resume her investigation. She accessed HOA records going back to 1988, when the Hansens first started renting the house on Toyon. The actual owner was a real estate firm in San Francisco. Hum, that's suspicious, but she would leave that one for the FBI to investigate. As for the Hansens' telephone calls: sensitive phone calls, both incoming and outgoing, would be made using burner phones, so they couldn't be traced. Only by bugging the home, Thelma thought, could we overhear any conversation whatsoever. Ultra savvy in spying, the Hansens would know immediately if we bugged their home. Any other surveillance would have to be done very carefully, for the same reason. Neither the FBI nor the CIA wanted the Hansen men to vanish. If they did suddenly leave, by the time the cameras were scanned, it would be too late to stop them.

* * *

That night, Thelma called Greg to ask him not to inform Colton of any of their findings from now on. "He may be romantically involved with Lena and he could mess up our investigation."

"All right, I understand," he said, "but what about Emily?"

"I think it would be best not to tell her anything more from now on, either."

"OK."

Thelma appreciated that this would be difficult for Greg. She knew that he was close to Emily and that Colton was Emily's son. But if Greg said he wouldn't tell Emily, Thelma knew he wouldn't.

The Good and the Bad

In an unexpected development in the Hansen case, Thelma Lee received a phone call from Mr. Carmichael at General Atomics. "Detective Lee, I have what I think might be significant information regarding our former employee whom we talked about two weeks ago." Mr. Carmichael asked Thelma to come to his office with discretion: plainclothes, no police car, etc.

"The detective force always dresses in plain clothes, Mr. Carmichael and we never drive police cars, so don't worry. When do you want to meet?"

"As soon as possible!"

"I'll be there in a half hour, maybe sooner."

"Thank you so much."

When Thelma walked into the main lobby, a uniformed man walked up to her before she even went through security. "Excuse me, ma'am, may I ask you what your name is?"

"Thelma Lee."

"May I see some identification?"

Normally, Thelma would have shown the man her business card, but Mr. Carmichael had stressed the need for discretion, so she showed him her driver's license instead.

"Please come with me, Miss Lee." He took her around a couple of corners to a small elevator, not the one used by most people, she thought.

Mr. Carmichael was at his office door. He beckoned her inside and shut it. "Detective Lee, I am embarrassed that I didn't know this when we spoke two weeks ago, but it just came to my attention this morning that we have another employee living at the same address as Lena Hansen. His name is Steve Hansen. He is a mechanical engineer in our drone division. His listed address is the same as hers. Perhaps he's her son. Of course, I am concerned that he may also be involved in espionage work."

"Are you planning on letting him go?"

"Yes, But I thought it would be right to let the police know first. I'm afraid now there is no way to keep this quiet. But we can't afford to have him steal any material. From what I hear, he is excellent, very bright and creative. I apologize for not telling you this sooner. I don't know all our people. I rely on the heads of various departments."

"Yes, I understand. I appreciate your informing me. I am embarrassed that we hadn't come across this information in our own investigation. We looked into the employment of the other members of the Hansen household. I don't know how this could have been overlooked."

"It's probably because that division has a separate name, 21st Technology, not General Atomics. You see, we acquired the firm eleven years ago, but kept its name the same."

"Oh, OK, that explains it."

Thelma knew she wasn't entitled to get help from Phil, even though they were working on the same case. Phil wouldn't be allowed to share with her information that he uncovered relevant to the case. When she phoned him to tell him that she had learned that Steve Hansen was working for a branch of General Atomics with a different name, his response was tepid. He must have known already and hadn't told her. She knew that's how the FBI operated. It wasn't an equal partnership, in fact, not a partnership at all. "If General Atomics terminates Steve, don't you think, the Hansen men will disappear?"

"Yes, I do, but what evidence we have will not be sufficient to convince a jury that the Hansens killed Katya Drozdov. We also can't stop General Atomics from letting Steve Hansen go."

"I understand. General Atomics doesn't want to be burned twice. You can't blame them."

* * *

Greg was now feeling awkward. As an HOA board member, he should let the board know that there was a major problem with the Hansen house.

The good news was that once the homeowners had read the scuba divers' report, many seemed more relaxed and were ready to once again enjoy the beauty of the lakes. They had heard that the lining appeared to be fine. They saw that the water was clearer and that the turtles' carapaces looked healthy again, black, and not peeling. There were a few trout still alive.

At the next board meeting, members expressed an interest in putting more fish in the lakes. However, President Marco was adamant that first, the water should be tested one more time. The plant contingent wanted more plants put in. Some complained about the swarms of midges. Others warned that insects have decreased worldwide. "9% decline per decade," Morgan called out.

Greg wished he could say that there was a Russian spy ring operating in their midst, just to shut them all up. Every now and then, he locked eyes with Emily. He planned to go to her house after the meeting for some welcomed diversion. The door opened and a young man, oh my God, Steve Hansen, entered and took a seat next to Emily. He was too late to make a public comment. The last homeowner to speak was just wrapping up: "And one last thing, does anybody know who put the drones in the lower lake?" Steve Hansen's eyes were on Greg. "It's bad enough that some outsiders don't pick up after their dog or just drop a McDonalds bag on the footpath, but now they're using our lakes as a trash bin."

When Greg walked into Emily's home after the meeting, he found out that Colton had just received a call from Thelma, reporting that the DNA of the skeleton in Mission Trails Park matched perfectly with that of Katya Drozdov. Thelma warned him that the news was going to go public in a day. "After that, reporters from all the local newspapers, and probably some national ones, will be ringing your doorbell and calling you on the phone for an interview."

Emily noticed Colton's spirits really picked up after Thelma's call. She was sure that Colton had long given up hoping that Katya was still alive. At least now he and Katya's Russian friends could have closure. They were all convinced that Vladimir Putin had ordered the assassination. "This news will cause Russians to discuss her murder in public again. That's good."

Colton went on to explain that there were some independent newspapers still operating in Russia. "They don't have large circulations, but Katya's body being discovered will be reported, in spite of the fact that most Russians get their news from television, and that much of the media is not neutral. Most are either censored by the government or self-censored."

Greg wanted to ask what 'self-censored' meant, but he didn't have a chance. Colton was having a talking jag. He looked at Emily. She appeared delighted, so pleased to see her son animated.

"Putin's party—United Russia—is by far the largest party in the country, but other parties exist. Russia has a capitalist economy now, and it is globally integrated with the rest of the world. Citizens can travel and speak more freely. However, elections are not free or fair. The voices of Putin's opponents are suppressed. Sometimes they're thrown in jail on trumped-up charges to keep them from running an effective campaign. Political critics of Putin's regime have been tortured, even assassinated. Russia is not a democracy, but it's closer to being one than in the days of the Soviet Union."

* * *

At 7:00 the next morning, Mr. Offenbacher went out to pick up his paper and noticed a white van with no markings had backed into the Hansen's driveway with the garage door open. He didn't think much of it, but by late afternoon, he heard a cat meowing outside his doorway. The ID tag on its collar said 'Felice,' with the next door's address. Frank assumed that the cat had got out of the Hansen house by mistake. He gave it some milk. Then he realized George's car was still parked out in front of the house. Had he not gone to work, he wondered?

That night, Frank looked for light coming from the Hansen home, but there was none. In the morning, Felice was again meowing on his doorstep. George's car was still in front of the house. Frank did not want to get involved with the Hansens, but he was worried that something might be wrong. He knocked on their door, but there was no answer. He went home and called Greg to ask for his advice.

By 4:00 in the afternoon, Thelma learned that the house had been vacated. The FBI camera showed the driver of the white van never got out, but, within minutes, George and Steve were seen getting into it with a few suitcases. Phil called Thelma to tell her the news. "The entire clip on the film took no more than 5 minutes," he said.

The front door was shut but not locked. A swarm of FBI agents combed the house for clues and evidence. Thelma didn't know what they had found. It was 10:00 that night when SDPD was finally permitted to search, with the understanding that "nothing could be removed from the house." The agents had left the keys to both cars on the dining table, so after her thorough search of the house, Thelma began her search of the two cars. She took out the mat in the trunk of George's car, where she found a strand of hair in the groove running parallel to the edging. She found another shorter strand caught on the edge of the rim of the trunk light. Since the car was not in 'the house,' Thelma didn't think it was too wrong for her to confiscate the two strands of hair for a lab analysis. Jim faithfully documented her findings.

Wait a minute, she told herself. What the hell! This was a murder investigation. Of course, the police have the right to impound the car when we think the victim was carried in it. Gees, those Feebs aren't in control of everything!

* * *

Neighbors wondered what was causing all the commotion going on at the Hansen house: unmarked cars parked all day outside, and people going in and out. Then at night, a police car was seen. An officer inspected George Hansen's car and, finally, a police tow truck took it away. This news was passed down Toyon Drive and beyond by the end of the next day.

By 10:30 the next morning, three reporters had asked for interviews with Colton. They took pictures of him, and sometimes of Emily, and even of the Quietwater lakes. "Someone killed Katya Drozdov, and she was last seen walking around these beautiful lakes."

Over the next several days, other newspapers and magazines followed. Of course, they found in Colton a wealth of information. He said to his mother: "It's like teaching the first 5 classes of Russia 101 over and over again." Explaining Chechnya was the hardest. After 9/11, it didn't please people to hear that Islamic radicals got involved. Colton insisted that the reporters understood how that came about.

Two years ago, the newspapers and TV had reported that a Russian journalist disappeared, but now, they reported that she was definitely murdered and where her body had been found. In two days time, most of the people in the community were reminded that the journalist had been visiting the Dunn family of Quietwater and that she was a close friend of Colton Dunn. Soon, Toyon Drive became the favorite destination of dogwalkers, instead of the lakes. People were taking photos of the Hansen house, or of their family in front of the Hansen house. Quietwater kids started begging their parents for spy costumes for Halloween: boys and girls alike wanted black trench coats, black fedoras, and sunglasses.

* * *

Days later, Thelma had finally caught up on her sleep. A DNA analysis was being done on the strands of hair that she found in George's trunk. She had recovered her self-esteem as a detective and was feeling good about herself. It was then that she received a call from Greg who said that Colton was gone. "He has left home." He went on to explain that he was calling her from

Emily's house. "Emily is quite upset. She's in the other room and can't hear me. I don't want her to get more upset, but I thought you should know right away."

"You mean he has left home for good?" she asked.

"It appears so. Emily says that Colton received a postcard this morning. He stood staring at it for a good two minutes, she said. Then he 'smiled like he used to when he was a boy,' is how she put it. Then, he briefly showed the postcard to Emily, just long enough for Emily to see that it was written in Russian. She said there was no signature. He took the postcard to his room and shut the door."

"Did Emily see the postmark?" Thelma asked.

"No, I'm afraid not. Then, Emily said, he started doing a lot of things in his room. When he finally opened his door, Emily was in the kitchen, so she didn't see him, but she thought he went into the garage. Later she realized that he was probably fetching suitcases.

"The next time he opened his bedroom door he emerged with two heavy suitcases and took them to his car. She kept asking him what he was doing. After he took the last load to his car, he answered her: 'Mom, trust me. I'll be gone a long time, maybe for years, and I won't be able to contact you. I love you. Say goodbye to Greg.' And he drove off."

Thelma took a moment to think about what she had heard, then she told Greg: "I don't think we have any justification to stop him. What kind of a car does he drive?"

"It's blue, dark blue, Japanese car—Nissan, I think." Greg realized that Emily had quietly entered the room. "Do you know the year?" he asked her.

"He bought it new three years ago," Emily answered.

Realizing that Emily was present, Thelma asked Greg if she could speak to her. "Emily, do not worry. Colton is a grown man and very intelligent. He has probably thought for a long time about this. He knows what to do. I know this is upsetting for you…. Emily, who do you think sent Colton the postcard?"

"I'm not positive, but the only person I can think of would be Lena Hansen."

* * *

Thelma had to report this both to her captain and to Phil. She had no choice. Greg would know it was her duty. She called Phil.

"Lots of thoughts," he said. "Maybe they're enticing Colton somewhere so they can use him as a hostage. I think we had better get right on to following him. I'll go now so I can get that started." Phil hung up.

Later, Phil called her back. "They're all slipping away," he lamented.

"Any sign that the Hansen men were in contact with Lena?"

"No. We have no way of knowing. It's possible by using burner phones, but we can't know for sure. At least we do have pictures of all three of them."

Later in the day, Colton was on the FBI's radar, so to speak, making his way east on Interstate 10. Thelma knew not to pass any of this on to Emily or Greg.

* * *

The next day, Phil called Thelma. "Well, we had two FBI agents following the blue Nissan with the right license number going east on I-10. You're not going to believe this. They continued following for another hour. The car left the freeway at exit 7, which put them in the town of Earl. The car made several turns before pulling into the driveway of a home at 680 Spring Street. A man got out of the car, and our agent says: 'Wait a minute, he doesn't look like Colton Dunn at all. What's going on?' Colton must have gotten rid of his car right away, traded it for another.

"Two hours later, one of the agents called me saying: 'Hey, I'm sorry, but we've lost him and have no idea what kind of a car he's driving now. We can't even be sure he's headed east.'"

"Would he know to switch cars on his own? Isn't he a nerdy intellectual type? To slip away from the FBI, I mean it's not like the guy watches cop shows on TV religiously."

Thelma could hear Phil pouring himself a cup of coffee. "Just got to add some sweetner." Thelma thought, typical man, can't add sugar and talk at the same time. "Of course the big question is: why is Colton being secretive?"

Thelma said: "The obvious answer is, as his mother says, that he's in love with Lena Hansen. He wants to keep her location secret, for her safety."

"But is that what Colton wants us to think? Maybe he's been recruited. Then the cell could continue to operate, even if the Hansen men are back in Russia." There was a long pause before he went on. "One thing that bothers me: from the Russians' point of view, the cell was compromised as soon as Lena left it—compromised, that is, if her leaving was not planned."

"I'm not with you. What do you mean?" Thelma asked.

"Well, if Lena's escape took the Hansen men by surprise, they would be expected to inform Moscow immediately. Then, most likely, Moscow would get the men out of San Diego and back to Russia."

"Has it occurred to you that maybe they didn't want to go back, so they didn't tell Moscow?" Thelma interjected.

"No, no, no. It doesn't work that way. George and Steve knew that if they didn't tell Moscow as soon as Lena left, they would be taken to Russia at once and killed. By telling Moscow, they would at least be assured a pen-pushing job in Kamchatka."

"But," Thelma injected, "two years have gone by and the men didn't seem alarmed. This makes me think that Moscow knows Lena is gone and it is trying to find her to kill her."

"Or," Phil remarked, "the cell has deliberately metastasized, with Colton duped by the woman and in on the plan."

"Well," Thelma said, "It doesn't look like the Russians have found Lena yet, and Colton's mysterious departure indicates she's still alive. She must be deeply hidden."

"If the Russians can't find her, probably we can't either."

* * *

Thelma called Mr. Carmichael at General Atomics to warn him that Steve would not be going to work that day. "I can't give you an explanation, but I have a favor to ask of you. It would save us a lot of time if you could have a couple of your drone design engineers come to Quietwater to look at the three drones that were pulled from the lake here…."

"Lake? You pulled them from a lake? There's a lake in Clairemont?"

"Yes, the development, the HOA, has two little lakes."

"I've never heard of them."

"Evidently, few people have. Anyway, the drones are being held, actually locked up, in the racquetball court. These are drones that Steve Hansen made in his garage, we think."

"Oh boy, this is not good."

Mr. Carmichael called Thelma a couple of hours later. "Detective Lee, I have two engineers from our drone design division who can go to Quietwater anytime, in fact, one is a resident of Quietwater."

This revelation not only surprised Thelma, but she found it discouraging. Good grief, she thought, could this mean another person in Quietwater is spying on General Atomics? The last thing Thelma wanted was for the case to get more complicated.

An hour later, she and the two engineers met Greg in front of the community center. With keys in his hand, Greg led them to the door of one of the racquetball courts. No windows for anyone to peek in through, Thelma thought, the court was a good place to stash the drones. Greg turned on the room's bright lights. There, in a corner of the court, were three black aircraft. "They're made of aluminum," Mr. Campbell said quietly, not expecting anyone but Gabriella to be interested. Thelma, however watched the two engineers closely as they inspected the drones.

"I'm surprised they're not more oxidized," Miss Rossi said. She looked up at Greg and Thelma to ask: "How long do you think these were in the lake?" They told her that they didn't know. "Well, I'd say not more than a couple of years. What do you think, Art?" She inspected them closely again. "I knew they had to be small."

Mr. Campbell spoke quietly to Miss Rossi. Thelma was only pretending not to listen. He said: "What an innovative design. Four rotary blades would allow it to take off vertically. No runway would be necessary."

"Yes," Rossi confirmed, "however, its range and speed wouldn't be as great. Hmm, but it could have many interesting applications." In a loud, clear voice, Miss Rossi asked Thelma if General Atomics could have the drones after the police were through with them.

Thelma told them that she would consider it, but that she couldn't promise. She knew she had heard the name of Art Campbell before. Oh, yes, he had been Lena's boss.

Thelma didn't ask them what they knew of Steve Hansen. She didn't want to reveal any information about the case that wasn't already public. She already knew Gabriella Rossi lived in Quietwater on Shoestring Acacia Drive.

The engineers kept asking Thelma questions, to which Thelma had to answer that she was not free to discuss the case. She thanked them several times for coming over and examining the drones. At a later time, she would be asking them more questions.

What Thelma had gleaned from the engineers' comments was that the drones were not copies of GA products, as she had expected. If Steve had made them, he was enjoying his freedom to experiment and be creative with the design.

The engineers left. Thelma lingered around Greg while he locked up the racquetball court. She wanted to ask him a question that had been bothering her but had nothing to do with the case. "What kind of a developer names a street Shoestring Acacia Drive?"

"It grows on you. We like to make nicknames. That street becomes Shoestring, Lemonade Berry Drive is just Lemon, Aleppo Pine Drive is just Leppo."

"I see," said Thelma. She thought: fun for Quietfarters.

Library Notice

Emily went into Colton's room to see what he had taken away with him. Maybe he left a clue as to where he was going. Her search turned out to be futile. There were piles of books that he hadn't taken. The little telephone was gone, as was Lena's photograph.

It took a while for it to sink in that Colton was really gone. He had always been so quiet, shut away in his room.

Long before Colton left, Greg and Emily had discussed what they would do once he was gone. A week later, Greg moved into her house. They planned to make Colton's room into an office. Their first job was to organize the numerous books he left behind. Before putting them in boxes labeled: 'Russian Literature,' 'Russian Language,' etc., they removed the bookmarks, notes, and flyers that he had left inside them.

"Do you think he's called the university to let them know he's not coming back to teach?"

"Sure. He wouldn't just leave without letting them know."

"What if there are things in his office that he'll want?"

"Maybe he went there and cleared all that up before leaving."

"What about his bank account, bills?...Actually, I don't think he has any bills. He paid cash for everything, even his car, you know."

"He's probably saved a fortune having lived at home all these years."

"Why couldn't he tell me where he was going?"

"Maybe he worried you would disapprove."

"It makes me feel like I don't know him, and that makes me sad. I always wanted to know him well. I wanted to be close, as other parents are."

Greg had made them some coffee. They took a break and sat down on the couch to drink it. "Emily, you have to accept him as he is. He's self-contained. He loves you, respects you, but just doesn't need you. I'm sorry. I know that hurts, but you have to move on. The thing that worries me is that he has possibly fallen in love with a spy, someone trained to be duplicitous. Is she going to lead him into the same type of dangerous, even traitorous career? Or drop him after she gets what she wants from him?"

Emily rested her head on Greg's shoulder and said: "He's embarked on an adventure, hasn't he? That was something I had always hoped for, that he would have some adventure in his life. I need to give him space."

Later in the morning, Emily pulled out an envelope from a book. "Oops, what's this? Here's a letter from the public library that was never opened. It's probably a notice that a book is due." She opened the envelope. "Oh, my goodness, this is strange. Look at this." She handed the notice to Greg to read.

"*Death of a Journalist* by VP Rast is reserved between June 15 and June 29, 2002."

"What's the date on the postmark?"

"June 13, 2002," Emily answered.

"Is it a threat or a warning?"

"Oh, it must be a warning, but Colton never opened the letter. That's not like him."

"Maybe he just stuck it in a book and thought he'd come back to it, but forgot about it."

"He rarely took out books from the public library, now that I think about it. He could get any book he wanted through the university. Should we show it to Thelma Lee?"

"Yes, I think we should."

"Have you ever heard of the last name of Rast?" Emily asked, following Greg as he was carrying a box of books to the garage. He was distracted and probably hadn't heard her question. If the title of the book was a warning, she thought, maybe the last name of its author was too. She reversed the letters: Tsar. "Greg!" Emily shouted. "Greg, it's definitely a warning."

In the kitchen fixing lunch together, Greg said: "'VP' probably stands for something, too."

Emily had already thought about it. 'Vice President' was her first thought, but that didn't make sense. Then it came to her: *Vladimir Putin.*

* * *

Things were starting to make sense to Thelma. She called Phil to share what had been brought to light: the hair found in George's trunk, which definitely belonged to Katya, and the library notice warning that Katya was going to be murdered. She had expected him to be embarrassed that the FBI hadn't found Katya's hairs in the trunk. But his response was just: "Damn, that evidence might have been sufficient to make a case against the Hansen men stick. Now we don't know where they are."

"I was thinking about that Phil, I think they have to be back in Russia."

"How's that?"

"I don't know if the U.S. has an extradition treaty with Russia, but even if we do, the Hansens could not be extradited because they have taken refuge in the country to which they are nationals. So, Russia wouldn't be required to turn them over to us. Isn't that right?"

"Yes, but how does that indicate that they are in Russia?" Phil asked her.

"They are protected if they are in Russia, so in my mind, that is where they would definitely want to be."

"Good thinking. OK, I'm convinced," Phil said.

Even if Phil didn't say so, Thelma had already solved, to her satisfaction, the Katya mystery. In her opinion, the Hansen men had definitely killed Katya. Now, the case had been reduced in scope to the Lena-Colton mystery.

Thelma thought about posing some of her other questions to Phil, to see if he had ideas that she hadn't thought of. But she sensed he wasn't very interested in the case anymore. She decided that she would have to pursue its solution on her own. The traditional FBI approach required much more money to solve a crime than was available to the SDPD. They had numerous agents to draw on, agents from all over the country. They could quickly throw lots of bodies at a task. That works well for many types of cases, she supposed, but this case called for a different approach. It was important to get into the minds of Lena and Colton, because now, there was not much else to go on.

She noticed Phil quickly attributed evil intent to Lena, once he knew she was a spy. She had heard him say such things as: "She escaped to save her own neck;…She's trying to turn Colton into being a spy;…She is using Colton to obtain legitimacy;… She's going to use Colton…." First, figure out who Colton and Lena are as people, how they tick as individuals—a challenge Thelma could meet more easily, due to her proximity, and maybe, because she was a woman.

DETECTIVE WORK

San Diego police detectives supposedly only worked four days a week, but those four days usually had at least twelve working hours each. As much as she needed a rest and a change on that fifth day, there were times when Thelma used it for police work. Those were the times when she was so involved in a case that she couldn't let it go. This was one of those times. She was always thinking about it. Working on the Lena-Colton case on her day of rest had the advantage of not having to let the others at the station know what she was doing.

Her extra day off was a Monday. That gave her a three-day weekend—a privilege her seniority among detectives granted her. For the first Monday in July, Thelma had made an appointment with the head of the Russian Studies Department at UCSD, Dr. Froshenka.

Dr. Froshenka's office was in the Humanities and Social Sciences Building on Gilman Drive. Since detectives never drove police cars, Thelma was at a disadvantage in her present situation. If she were in a police car, she would have been able to drive right up to the building and park in front of it. Now she had to find a visitors' parking place. She asked a young Asian-looking man where to find one. He was strapped into a backpack and was hurrying somewhere—actually, all the students were hurrying somewhere.

"Oh sorry, yes. Ah, the few for visitors go quickly. You might try way over in that far corner," he said while pointing across the immense parking lot.

By the time Thelma opened the door to Room 1024, she was

late for her appointment. She hated being late. The secretary escorted her to Dr. Froshenka's office. The department head was a small man, both in stature and frame, with a gray mustache. His scalp appeared stretched taut over his skull, with just a valance of curly hair to tickle his neck.

After introductions, Thelma asked her first question: "How was Colton Dunn's position in Russian Studies terminated?"

"It was sudden and much regretted," Dr. Froshenka answered.

Thelma realized her question was abrupt. She was agitated about being late. She tried to calm down. She saw how relaxed Dr. Froshenka was. "When did he first speak to you about it?" she asked him.

"Oh dear, Colton is not in trouble is he?"

"No, no," Thelma assured him. She needed to calm down. The man is nice, co-operative, direct, even forthcoming, she told herself.

"Colton appeared to be having a mid-life crisis, ten years in advance of most of us," he chuckled. "I didn't see it coming nor did his colleagues, from what they tell me."

"Would you mind describing the sequence of events?"

"Yes, let's see, he made an appointment in May." Dr. Froshenka had a large spiral notebook that served as his calendar. "Here it is, I think. It looks like it has been erased for some reason, but I can see a faint impression that it was June 4."

Thelma took out a notepad and recorded the date. Another disadvantage of working on her day off was that Jim was not with her to help her take notes. "Had the appointment been changed?" she asked.

"No. I remember it now because it was the day before my wife's birthday."

"What did he come to talk to you about?"

"He apologized for the sudden notice, but he said he would not be able to teach in the fall.... He was afraid he was having an emotional breakdown. 'I have to do this for myself,' he said."

"Did this emotional disorder show up in his teaching?"

"I asked that of his colleagues in the department and they said no. He has always received high marks for his teaching, handed in grades on time. Yes, he seems to have always met the deadlines. The students liked him. He was a bit of a loner, but his career was progressing nicely."

"What about friends? Any close friends in the department?... female friends?"

"No." A glimmer of a smile crossed Dr. Froshenka's face.

"Do you think he was gay?"

"I wondered at one point, but I never saw any indication. In fact, that was what was unusual about Colton. He didn't have an attraction to anybody...truly a loner, but pleasant."

"Did he clear out his office?"

"Yes, I think he cleared it out right after he came to speak to me. Anyway, it's since been turned over to another professor."

Thelma did a quick calculation. The DNA match of the body in Mission Trails Park went public on May 28. Therefore, Colton must have decided to go away after there was proof that Katya had been murdered, but before he had received the postcard. Perhaps he wanted to make it look like the postcard had initiated his leaving, Thelma thought.

A week later, Thelma learned from Greg that Emily had seen a cell phone in Colton's room. "Emily just told me about it," Greg said.

"Did it have a bag or case that could be a Faraday shield?" Thelma asked. Greg answered that he had never seen the phone or any jacket, and Emily had no idea when he asked her about it. Thelma didn't comment to Greg, but she was beginning to think that secrecy was a pattern in Colton's behavior. Why?

* * *

Thelma called Phil and told him about her latest findings. As they spoke, there was something else she thought the FBI could help her with. "Her real name is Lena Yurin."

"Yes." He was drinking something. He was dreading being asked a favor. She could hear it in his voice.

"Just hear me out," Thelma continued. "Lena is probably trying to hide from the Russians who see her as a traitor. She knows the Russians know her real name is Lena Yurin, right?"

"Yes, but the FBI's searched for her as Lena Yurin, too, if that's what you're leading up to."

"Yes, I did want to check on that, but I was sure that you all would have searched for Lena Yurin. Here's the thing—Lena would not be able to use a passport or drivers license to leave the country, to register at a motel, or to get a new driver's license using the name of Lena Yurin, because the Russians, like the FBI, would be checking that name. She obviously can't use the name Hansen. So what name would she use?"

"Beats me! She could use anything; Smith, Jones, who knows?"

"She can't use any identity document that she has to leave the country or set up residence on her own in the U.S. She has no friends or relatives she could move in with."

"You're right. She's in a jam."

"Who would be willing to take her in without knowing her?"

"Thelma, I'm not up for speculations like these, I have too much to do. We don't have enough to go on. We can't go on without something more concrete."

"I agree, Phil. I could lay it down, if I just knew where she was born and under what name. Remember how you were able to obtain the Russian names of the Hansens?"

"Yes, but the CIA handled that task."

"Oh yeah. Do you think you could ask your friend there to make this one last inquiry? Please, then I'll be off your back."

"OK, I will, but it's going to take time."

"Thanks, Phil. Say Hi to Linda."

"Gees, she's been after me to arrange another camping trip with you. Yah, I'd better get this info to you first, otherwise we'll be sitting around the campfire discussing Russian spies."

* * *

That night, after she had her dinner, Thelma gave Greg a call. He was an old friend, and in his day, he was a crackerjack detective. There may be something that might occur to him that she had overlooked. She knew she shouldn't ask her questions without reviewing for him the significant events and the order in which they occurred.

"Sure, I'll try to help. Send me both the timeline and your questions? Email is fine."

Date	Event/Questions
1996–2001	drones spotted over Quietwater at night
1998	Colton meets Lena
09/28/01	Lena fired from General Atomic
Nov. 2001	burner phone & Lena's photo in Colton's room
06/28/02	Katya murdered Lena disappears (why? to where?)
05/18/04	skeleton found in Mission Trails Park
05/28/04	public learns skeleton's DNA matches Katya's
05/31/04	discovered that Steve works for GA
06/01/04	Hansen men vanish (back to Russia?)
06/04/04	Colton resigns from teaching at UCSD
06/06/04	postcard arrives (who sent? why show to Emily?) Colton leaves - slips FBI

Thelma sent the above timeline with a note that said: "I hope something occurs to you. Sleep well, my friend, Thelma."

* * *

On a later Monday, Thelma made an appointment to interview Art Campbell at General Atomics, Lena's immediate boss. In talking with Mr. Campbell, Thelma felt he was bitter that

Lena had been deceitful to him. "I let her bring her dog to work, for God's sake." Mr. Campbell wanted to know which company benefitted from Lena's theft. "I bet it was Lockheed Martin."

"I'm sorry I don't know. Is there someone at General Atomics who would know more about Lena Hansen? Is there someone else I should talk with?" Thelma asked.

"Yes, perhaps you should talk with Gabriella Rossi."

"OK, I remember her. She's the design engineer who came to Quietwater with you to examine the drones."

That same afternoon, Thelma had a chance to question Miss Rossi. Interviews of people on their own turf told Thelma so much more than those conducted at the police station. Being on the floor with the design engineers gave Thelma the feel for their working conditions. People here, she concluded, seemed relaxed, yet intent on their work.

Miss Rossi spoke very fast, mixing jokes with serious comments. Too bad Jim wasn't with her. Thelma found it impossible to write fast enough and listen at the same time. The most pertinent information she shared was that after she and Art inspected the drones, it occurred to her that the rose petals that she had found on her doorstep several years prior were probably delivered by the guy who dumped the drones in the lake.

Thelma asked why she thought that. "Well," she said laughing, "most of the petals were put on my doorstep, but I remember wondering why, on that windless day, I found some petals on the bushes, on the street, even some on the deck in the back of my house. I repeat: there was no wind! What had worried me was how the prankster got to the back deck, because I keep the gate to the backyard padlocked." Miss Rossi wanted to know if Thelma knew who that person might be.

Thelma couldn't tell her that it was probably Steve Hansen. She simply answered that she didn't know. Thelma was quite sure, however that Miss Rossi didn't believe her. "Well, it was nice, but creepy—mostly creepy."

* * *

Meanwhile, Greg and other HOA board members had to deal with all the sudden publicity Quietwater was receiving. Many homeowners were not pleased that "outsiders" were driving through their community looking for the 'Hansen house.' In so doing, they were getting lost, discovering the beauty of the lakes, and from then on, it was feared, making Quietwater a weekly destination for family outings.

Public comments at the HOA board meeting were lively, and, of course, controversial: "We must gate our community to keep these people out."

"Having people see our community raises property values."

"Gating will raise our property values."

"Look at what this publicity has done for us. We're now known throughout San Diego."

"Yeah, as a quiet place for murder."

"Spy haven!"

Greg was scheduled to retire from the board. He couldn't wait. At the same time, he enjoyed being part of a community of middle-class people who had no cause, no ideology, no religion in common. They had to cooperate enough to govern themselves. There were people who, without being asked, donated their time and labor to improve the community or to help a neighbor in need.

Waiting

Months went by and Thelma hadn't heard from Phil, but she didn't waste the time while she was waiting. She considered Lena's interests—the little she knew about them. There were two that she had heard about: plants and Chechnya. She tackled Chechnya first because that was also an interest of Colton's.

Thelma thought she had better find out more about that country. She spent a couple of Mondays at the Central Library downtown reading articles. She recalled that Katya Drozdov was famous for her investigative reporting on the wars there. All three had a strong interest in Chechnya. Why Lena? Of course! Thelma remembered Colton telling her that she might be able to get a good sample of Lena's DNA from a book about Chechnya in the Central Library. She had to be Chechen.

How did Lena acquire the surname of Yurin which is definitely a Russian name? If she was born in Chechnya, to Chechen parents, her name was likely to be Chechen, not Russian.

Phil was right when he accused her of speculating. That was what she was doing, but she was encouraged. Through speculation, some of the puzzle pieces were starting to fit together. A month later, she had another hunch: if Lena fled and had to find a stranger who would take her in, it would likely be a Chechen. Following up on this guess she tried to get an estimate for the number of Chechens living in the United States and their likely locations. From what she read, it was, at most, 250 individuals. Thelma couldn't find one official organization, not even an online community of ethnic Chechens living in the U.S.

Why so few? It was a small group of people, even before the

wars, and those wars devastated their country. Most Chechen refugees were far too poor to seek refuge in a place that required crossing an ocean to get to. In the last five years, Islamic extremists had been trying to radicalize Chechens, and the U.S. had become much more restrictive as to who was allowed to enter the country. 9/11 did no favors to Chechens wanting entrance.

An immigrant tracking agency informed Thelma that the families that had settled in the United States were widely dispersed: Boston, New Jersey, Washington, D.C., and Los Angeles, and that they were not likely to be in contact with each other.

Months went by, and she was so busy with other work that she hadn't had much time to devote to it. When she finally did have some time, she thought she would look for prominent Chechens. Maybe there were some who came to the U.S., either before or during the wars. Such people may have some good suggestions for her. Thelma's search yielded three prominent Chechen immigrants: Umar Tsatieva, Baiev Khassen, and Sulim Israilov.

Through inquiries over the phone, Thelma learned Umar Tsatieva was teaching at Antioch College, in Yellow Springs, Ohio. Yellow Springs was supposedly a charming little town, a liberal enclave in a conservative region of the state. The college itself was small, really small, only 100 students, mostly conscientious hippies with environmental leanings. Umar was a possibility, but it's hard to hide in a small town. Eventually, you know everyone and everyone knows you.

Thelma learned that Baiev Khassen was a surgeon living with his family in Needham, Massachusetts. His credentials were very impressive. In spite of a successful career in Moscow as a plastic surgeon, he returned to his native Chechnya in 1988 to help his fellow Chechens. His dedication was so well thought of that the Physicians for Human Rights group had sponsored him for political asylum in the United States.

Sulim Israilov had settled in the Arlington Heights region of Los Angeles. He had been a battalion commander in the Chechen army, and was noted for his bravery and clever tactics. When Thelma learned of him, he was living in a three-room apartment with his wife and four children. He drove a taxi to support his family. How they got from Grozny to Los Angeles was a mystery.

Thelma thought Baiev Khassen would be the Chechen Lena would most likely choose to ask for help. Would such an honorable surgeon even consider helping a former Russian spy? Probably not, but Thelma might learn something from him that would produce another lead she could follow to help her discover the whereabouts of Lena. Anyway, Thelma had already been planning to make the trip East in the spring of 2006, to see her sister Nancy in Northampton, Massachusetts. Maybe on that trip, she could find Dr. Khassen. This was such a long shot she was too embarrassed to tell anyone about her intentions. Now, what she needed was confirmation that Lena was Chechen. She knew not to bug Phil. She waited and waited for him to report back to her.

Finally, in February of 2006, Phil called Thelma to report. "Yes! Lena is Chechen by birth. Her surname was originally Vakhaev. Your guesswork paid off," Phil followed, expressing respect for her detective work. Thelma was overjoyed and thanked him accordingly.

Thelma knew she couldn't ask another favor of Phil, and she couldn't let her captain know that she was about to embark on another wild-goose chase. Baiev Khassen was the goose. There was no guilt because she would be doing the investigation while on vacation, visiting her sister.

She had better determine if Dr. Khassen was still living in Needham, Massachusetts, and at the same time, Thelma couldn't resist trying to also acquire more information about Lena. If Lena had a driver's license in the name of Lena Yurin, the FBI would have found it. So, Thelma used her police authority to search the Massachusetts Department of Motor Vehicles for the driver's license of Lena Vakhaev. An answer came back a day later that there was no such person registered with the DMV.

Thelma's heart sank. She shouldn't have been so optimistic. Stewing over this disappointment kept her awake much of the night. Maybe Lena hadn't moved to Massachusetts. Maybe she did settle there, but never applied for a MA driver's license. Maybe Lena got married and has a new last name. (Good thing her colleagues didn't know how far-fetching her thinking could take her.) Next morning, Thelma asked the DMV of Massachusetts to search again for the license of someone with the middle name of Vakhaev. This time she was expecting nothing. Three days later, she got a reply that there was a license issued to a Angelina Vakhaev Dunn.

DUNN! Thelma was ecstatic. Lena was married to Colton Dunn and now she calls herself Angelina. Wow, that was a big discovery! And Lena was likely to be living in Massachusetts. Just when Thelma made these discoveries, she was in the middle of a difficult case that required all of her attention for a week. That was probably just as well, because that gave her time to contemplate what she should do next.

My goodness, they're married. Well that answers one thing: Colton was drawn to Lena romantically, but did she marry him for convenience? Has she lured him into helping her continue the sleeper cell?

Immediately, the important question she had to answer was should she tell Greg? Greg knew she was still working on the case, but Emily didn't. She decided not to tell him until she knew for sure that she could locate the couple. Maybe Lena married Colton, got an address, a new passport, a new driver's license, and then murdered him. Horrible thought, but she better find out more before she raised the hopes of Greg and Emily.

The Massachusetts DMV sent a photocopy of Lena's license to Thelma. It arrived two days later. Thelma didn't recognize Lena—she was the right age, but her face seemed different. The address given was 301 Maple Street, Needham, MA. Was that the address of Baiev Khassen? An additional inquiry of the MS DMV generated an immediate email. Baiev Khassen's address was also registered at 301 Maple Street. Happy days!

Thelma didn't want to inform Phil of her discovery at this point. The approach of the FBI, she thought, would be adversarial. Thelma wanted to assess the situation first, before other people became alarmed. Colton would recognize her. Maybe she could get her sister Nancy to help.

FLIGHTS EAST

Emily heard a "creek, creek,…clink" outside of the house. She glanced up at the clock hanging on the living room wall. It's the letter carrier opening up the metal mail slot, stuffing the mail through it, and letting the flap drop shut. Should she get up? Rarely was there anything of interest in the mail. Greg was snoozing on the recliner. His book was open but resting upside down on his tummy. She usually didn't bother collecting the mail until the box was overflowing, but she had nothing to do at that moment. She quietly got up from her chair, opened the hall door to the garage, and brought the stack back to her chair.

In amongst the several ads and solicitations for donations to various causes, there was a small white envelope addressed to her, with no return address and a Massachusetts postmark. She thought she recognized Colton's handwriting.

She quickly tore open the envelope, telling herself not to be too hopeful. As she pulled out a white note folded in half, two small pictures tumbled out with it. One was of a baby. Emma Katya was written on the back. The other was of a three-year-old boy whose name must be Rasul Vakhaev because that was written on the back of his photo. "Greg!" She didn't know what nationality Rasul was. It was a name she had never heard of. Look at those eyebrows. They have to be from Colton. "Greg!" Emily burst out crying and shook Greg awake.

Days later, it occurred to them that Vakhaev was probably Lena's family name. From the internet they learned that Vakhaev was a Chechen surname. They were on the right track. From there, Greg used various tricks that he had had up his sleeve as a former detective of the San Diego Police Department and found the 301 Maple Street address in Needham, Massachusetts. Four days later, he and Emily were booked on a flight from San Diego to Boston.

* * *

The night before Thelma was due to fly East to visit her sister, she called Greg to ask him if he had any bright ideas after considering the timeline that she had emailed him. "No," he answered, "and you? Has anything occurred to you?"

"No. Phil keeps telling me to consider the cases closed."

"Yes, I suppose he's right."

* * *

When Thelma flew to Boston the next morning, it had been over two years since she had seen her sister. She rented a car so she could drive to Northampton. Every time she was in that city, it seemed to have grown bigger, but it still maintained its New England charm: lovely, tall shade trees and frame houses. She thought she had heard that Northampton had become a foodie hot spot.

The drive from Boston to Nancy's house had taken three hours. Thelma pulled up along the curb and was pleased to see that Nancy's magnificent magnolia tree was in bloom. Opening the car door, Thelma stood still for a moment to take in the wonderful fragrance. As she walked to the front door carrying her suitcase, she passed by Nancy's numerous azalea bushes with their dazzling pink and red blossoms. Then, she remembered the oddity of Nancy's azaleas: all that color and no scent.

Nancy was two years older than Thelma. She had always been the bright star in the Lee family. Ten years ago, she became a lawyer for Smith College in Northampton. Her husband Carl was a sweet man, although Thelma rarely had the opportunity to talk to him. They had three children: one problematic, one near perfect, but Suzy was neither and was Thelma's favorite.

Now that Thelma and Nancy's parents had passed, the two sisters had become closer, even though as people, they were quite different. Thelma had never married. She was attracted to men, but those she knew well, she valued more as friends. Solving problems and mysteries is what drove Thelma. To some people, her worst character trait was that she was incapable of deviating from whatever problem she was working on. No surprise that her appearance was usually secondary in importance. Thelma had many male friends, but their joking back and forth would never be described as flirting. She was a little overweight and didn't care because she knew she was stronger and more agile than most men her age. Her hair was brown and straight. She wore it pulled back into a ponytail, a will-do hairstyle.

Usually, Thelma travelled to visit Nancy rather than the other way around. It was easier that way. Thelma didn't have a family, making her more mobile, albeit 'incomplete,' in the eyes of some. But she was content with her life. Police work didn't lend itself easily to superficial casual conversation. That was OK, a little chatting went a long way with Thelma. Law enforcement was important work. Thelma was satisfied with her life.

Several days later, Thelma and Nancy drove together to Needham. The drive took two hours. They had little difficulty finding the house on Maple Street. The home was quite large.

Although Thelma was glad for her sister's company while driving, she wasn't sure she wanted Nancy to participate in the investigation, but she couldn't think of a polite way to ask her to stay in the car. Furthermore, if Colton were there in the house and saw Thelma, that would not be good. Having Nancy go in without her wouldn't work either, because Thelma had to be the one to assess the situation. So Thelma had to takes her chances. She and Nancy got out of the car and walked up to the front door together.

A metal plaque on the wall by the front door said: *The office of Dr. Baiev Khassen, surgeon.* Before pressing the doorbell, the sisters paused to take in the fact that they heard a baby cry. Thelma pressed the doorbell and was surprised by the chime, which was the opening notes of Beethoven's Fifth. The sisters chuckled. That whimsy must have prompted Nancy to ask how old Dr. Khassen was. Thelma explained that she had never met the man but she figured he was in his early sixties. "Nancy, I hope you are up for some playacting."

"Is that part of a detective's job?"

"Yes, every now and then."

Thelma almost rang the bell again, but a small gray-haired woman finally opened the door. She was holding a baby who went from tears to smiles in two seconds. After introductions, Thelma asked if she could speak to Dr. Khassen. "He's not here right now, but I can let you speak to his assistant. Come in won't you." She led them into a good-sized living room with a large Persian carpet placed on top of wall-to-wall carpeting.

"Please have a seat."

The room was lovely. Parts of the décor were unusual, even foreign to Thelma. Silk pillows, big and small, were on every chair and the couch. Nancy sat down on the couch but Thelma was too excited. She walked over to the large picture window that looked out on the backyard. There was a man out there tossing a big air-filled ball to a little boy, around three years old, Thelma thought. A small white dog was jumping up at the ball.

Thelma heard what must have been the assistant entering the room behind her but she was momentarily captivated watching the man with his shock of brown hair and bushy eyebrows playing with the boy. Suddenly, she realized the man was Colton. She whipped around and watched the assistant introducing herself to Nancy. Thelma became breathless and could barely say hello. My God, this woman could be Lena. She doesn't look like the picture I've seen. The wavy brown hair is short and much lighter, almost blond. The face is much rounder than Thelma remembered, and this woman does not have a hooked nose. She didn't match the photo. Thelma listened to the assistant's voice and detected a slight accent to her speech. Maybe this is actually just an assistant to the doctor and Lena is elsewhere in the house.

Looking at Nancy, the assistant was saying: "Dr. Khassen is at the hospital seeing a couple of patients. I'm not sure when he'll be back at the house. Would you like to make an appointment… for another day, perhaps?"

Nancy looked at Thelma, expecting her to reply. Thelma collected herself and said: "Yes, would he be free Thursday morning?"

"I'm sorry, Thursdays and Fridays are reserved for surgery." The assistant went to a desk in the corner which Thelma had not yet noticed, and consulted a large appointment book. "He is available on Tuesday.…"

Thelma made an appointment quickly. She didn't want Colton to walk in because he would surely recognize her.

"Miss Lee, can I let the doctor know for what reason you want a consultation?"

"Abdominal pains."

"And can I tell him who your primary care doctor is?"

"I'm sorry, I forget so much these days, Nancy can you remember his name."

"Dr. Patrick Sheridan," Nancy replied. "My sister has been staying with me." Nancy gave Lena a meaningful look. "I'll be coming here with her for her appointment next Tuesday." Another meaningful look passed between them. Lena gave Thelma a card with the date of the appointment. Nancy stood up. "Why don't you let me keep that in my purse?" Thelma, acting confused, handed the card to Nancy. "Well, come on, Sis, let's get you home."

When they were back in the car, Thelma thanked Nancy. "You were just great, a natural."

"Well, now can I hear what that was all about?"

"No, I'm afraid I can't say a thing."

"Oh, that's not fair."

"Sorry, Nancy, cloak-and-dagger rules, you know. I'll call up on Monday and cancel the appointment."

"At least tell me if you accomplished what you came for?"

"Yes, oh yes!" Thelma answered with a big smile.

"You have me intrigued. I had no idea detective work could be so much fun."

When they were back at Nancy's house in Northampton, her sister's attention became absorbed by her children. Thelma excused herself. She went to the guestroom where she was staying. She needed some time alone to think.

What should she do now that she knew where Lena was? Or was that Lena? Should she report her findings to Phil so the FBI could arrest her? She didn't have the heart to do that, especially since she wasn't sure the woman was actually Lena. They all looked so happy.

Could Lena accomplish anything criminal in her present situation? She's an assistant to a renowned doctor and happily married with two children.

Yet, people are supposed to be punished for their crimes. As a policewoman, she was supposed to follow the law. But no one would ever know if she neglected that duty, just this once, if they never discovered where Lena was. But again, the woman may not even be Lena.

One thing was clear: Thelma should let Emily know where her son was, that he was safe and happy. That she had to do. She thought for several minutes and finally decided to tell Greg. He can decide how to handle this situation. After all, he's retired. He can't be fired. She needed to let Greg know, in some way, that didn't reveal that she knew where Colton and…Angelina were.

She checked her watch. It's 3:00 in the afternoon here, so it must be noon in San Diego, Thelma reasoned. She picked up her cell phone and called Greg.

"Hi, Greg, it's Thelma …" She was going to continue by saying, 'I have some good news for you,' but he interrupted her.

"Sorry, Thelma, I'm going to have to call you back. I'm really busy right now."

Thelma heard the Beethoven's Fifth's chime in the background. "Ah, don't bother, Greg. It's nothing very important. I'll be home next week. Talk to you then." After hanging up, Thelma smiled.

Either that was just a monumental coincidence, or Greg was ringing Dr. Khassen's doorbell at this very moment!

* * *

Five days later, the day before Thelma was due to fly back to San Diego. Nancy wanted to show her Smith College's campus. "There are quite a few changes since you last saw it."

It was a beautiful campus. There were only a few large student dorms. They were arranged in a quadrangle. Most students' campus homes were in framed houses. The girls rode skateboards or bikes to classes. Thelma was very impressed by the new engineering building. Then she remembered what she loved most. "Can we walk around that pond again?" she asked her sister. "What was it called?"

"Paradise Pond—sure, let's go." They were both wearing jeans and sneakers. Thelma felt more relaxed than she had in years. It had been a good trip. She and Nancy had had long talks about their parents and childhood. It was lovely to feel such closeness again. As they walked on the path around the pond, Nancy told some stories of events and characters associated with the pond. At one point, they had stopped at the edge to watch a flock of Canada Geese. Nancy suddenly whispered: "Look!" She pointed to a tiny bird with blue and yellow coloring on an overhanging branch. "That is a Northern Parula," she said quietly. I've only seen one, once before, three years ago—it's one of the smallest warblers." They stood there for some time listening to its song.

"Sounds like a zipper," Thelma said laughing. She had forgotten how much Nancy loved birds. They continued walking. "I think I remember a swinging bench. Is that right—up on a hill?"

"Yes, yes, that's a lovely spot. I think it's just around the corner. Let's go there."

They walked by turtles and ducks on the bank near a bed of reeds. Rounding the corner, Thelma looked up the hill and spotted the swing. Amused by her own competitive spirit, she sped up so she could get to the swing before Nancy. "Uh oh." An old couple had crested the hill. Their line of descent aimed directly for the bench.

Thelma and Nancy both laughed. They had been walking for 45 minutes and hadn't seen a soul until then. It was a man and wife, probably. The way the man walked seemed familiar to Thelma. She knew that gait. As they got closer, Thelma and Nancy instinctively slowed down and smiled at each other, silently agreeing that age should have priority.

They continued to walk in that direction. "Oh my God, it's Greg—Greg and Emily," Thelma said. She picked up her pace. Nancy wasn't keeping up with her. "Greg," she shouted. So, he *was* ringing Dr. Khassen's doorbell, she said to herself.

"Thelma," Greg called back to her. His face appeared red, Thelma thought.

"What are you doing here?" she asked him. "Hi Emily."

"Oh, Emily wanted to show me her college." Introductions ensued.

"Is that right?" Nancy said. "What year were you in?"

"1960...."

Finally, Thelma asked Greg and Emily if they were enjoying their trip. Emily answered with great enthusiasm. They kept talking for minutes more before Thelma and Nancy said goodbye and continued walking up the hill.

* * *

Going over this encounter in her mind, Thelma realized that she and Greg had both reached the same decision: not to report Lena's whereabouts to the authorities. Was it Lena? Was Greg as conflicted as she was?

But during the five-hour flight back to San Diego, Thelma started having second thoughts. She kept wondering how Colton and Lena pulled this off, assuming for the moment that Angelina was Lena.

The postcard was puzzling. Did Lena send it? Colton had already made up his mind to not teach at UCSD before the postcard was delivered. He was prepared to leave, that explains why he could go so quickly.

If he wanted to protect Lena's hiding place, why did he even briefly show the card to his mother? Perhaps, for her sake, he wanted to soften the shock of his sudden departure by giving her a glimmer of a reason as to why he was leaving.

How did Colton know where to go? Thelma concluded that Colton and Lena had to have been in communication all along, but how? Their system must have been set up before she left San Diego, before Katya was murdered, maybe long before. They wouldn't have chosen a third party to deliver messages. That would be too risky as would mail to Colton's home or office at UCSD.

Colton could have opened a P.O. Box somewhere outside of San Diego. He would go to his box by taking the bus, not his car, which the Russians might have been tracking. The P.O. Box would have been set up long before Lena left San Diego. That was how she could send him her new address in Massachusetts.

Thelma was feeling good about her analysis, so much so that she thought she deserved a glass of wine. While sipping a Merlot, she allowed herself to fantasize even further.

As secure as their communication system sounded to Thelma, she could imagine that Lena would take the extra step of putting the messages she mailed to Colton in code. Years ago, Greg had told Thelma about pangrams—sentences that use all 26 letters of the alphabet, eg. *The quick brown fox jumps over a lazy dog.* Lena could have taught Colton how to decode her message using a pangram before she left.

She swallowed the last of the Merlot. There was only a half hour more of the flight before she landed in San Diego, and Thelma had not tackled her most difficult problem. She didn't want Lena to be arrested and jailed for espionage. It would mean years in federal prison. That would be devastating to their young family. Yet her duty as a cop was to report what she had discovered. She decided she would ask her captain for an hour of his time because she had something complicated, although not urgent, that she needed to discuss with him.

When that meeting came, she didn't have a chance to even start in on her explanation. Her captain said:

"Is this about the Lena Hansen case?"

"Yes, sir."

"You have to drop the case Thelma. I didn't know you were still working on it."

Thelma opened her mouth to explain and he interrupted her. "Drop it, Thelma. No questions, no explanations, and don't discuss it with anybody. Is that clear? I'm sorry to be abrupt with you, but I have to be."

"Yes, sir."

"You consistently do good work. I have always been pleased with your perseverance and imaginative analyses. But this case must...be...dropped. Now is there anything else you wanted to talk to me about?"

"No, sir."

On the one hand, Thelma was glad her boss had been so firm. If she can't say anything about Lena/Angelina, the Feds can't imprison her and the family stays intact. Why was the captain so adamant that the case be dropped? She thought he must have received an order from on top. Maybe Lena is continuing her spy work and the CIA/FBI is following it so they can catch other spies? No, Lena, as a mother with an unclassified job would be of little interest to Russian Intelligence. Maybe she turned, not recently, but long ago. Maybe Colton helped to turn her. STOP IT, THELMA, DROP THE CASE!

INTERSECTING PARALLELS

When Greg and Emily flew home to San Diego, they talked to each other quietly during the entire five-hour flight, excluding time for some dozing off now and then. Emily was overjoyed to see Colton again, and as a happily married man! That was more than she had ever hoped for, and grandchildren to boot! She couldn't have asked for more. She and Greg, at first, were uncertain that Angelina was actually Lena, the spy. Angelina looked like a different person than Emily had met years ago, and from the one in the photograph she had seen in Colton's room. She seemed a perfectly fine woman, a good mother, and there was no doubt in Emily's mind that she loved Colton.

"Baiev went on about Chechnya, didn't he?"

"Yes, that was fascinating," Greg responded. "He definitely insinuated that Angelina was born there. It must be a rock in Baiev's gullet to think of Angelina as a Russian spy, knowing, from what Colton told us, how much the Chechens hate Russians."

Greg paused, then blurted out: "The Khassen's are saints! My God, when you think of all that they've done for Angelina and Colton." Greg was trying to say Angelina and not Lena.

He thought back to a particular afternoon at the Khassen's when their families were seated outside on the terrace having tea—the best tea Greg had ever had! Baiev tried to explain to them why he and Yeza, his wife, were happy to do this. "Our most recent generation has grown up with war. They have had no social protection, yet I am confident this generation knows how to love, trust, and believe."

He turned to Lena. "You, my dear, were taken away to Moscow

so early—eight or ten, was it?"

"Ten," Angelina said.

"Well, before the wars, you had already lost your family. Then as a young adult, you were trained for espionage work. Even with all that, you recovered. You never forgot how to love. That is what is wonderful about the human spirit. Like you, Angelina, we must remember the children of the Chechen wars who are now awakening to adulthood. We must remember them, help them become aware of Chechen culture, a culture that has been forming for thousands of years…."

Greg told them that it was hard for him to imagine the horror of living under an invading force that decimated cities and left most people homeless and without food. "The tragedy of 9/11 pales in comparison."

"The West saw the Chechen conflict as merely an internal matter for Russia. By labeling it a domestic problem, there was no stopping Putin from victimizing not just those he labeled as terrorists, but the families and friends of those 'terrorists.' They were tortured as well. Our capital, Grozny, should never have been carpet bombed while it was full of civilian inhabitants. These crimes went unpunished.

"I'm afraid Putin will not stop with Chechnya. He'll see it as a green light to invade Georgia and Ukraine. They'll be next."

Greg didn't feel as knowledgeable as he perhaps should be, so he didn't contribute when the conversation went political. But he and Emily were feeling guilty that the Khassens were helping Angelina and Colton so much. He tried to have a frank conversation with Baiev when they were alone.

Greg told him: "I think the Russians are searching for Angelina with the intent of killing her."

"Yes, that is what she has said, right from the day she first arrived here."

"She told you then that she had been a Russian spy?"

"Yes, yes, she told us her whole story right away. She helped us cook and clean. Of course, she couldn't go out of the house.

She was too scared. She did once the baby was born, though. A year later, she started shopping and running errands for us. She paid us, too, bought most of the baby equipment herself. The timing worked out fine. Both of our children were out of the nest. This house is bigger than it appears. We have five bedrooms and three-and-a-half baths. Besides, Yeza and I have been through a lot in our earlier years. We've lived through many episodes of chaos and danger."

Greg kept saying to himself—they did all this for a perfect stranger. "We would like to arrange for them to live on their own, to give you relief."

"I think they are ready to go, but do you think it will be safe for them? I know you are in law enforcement."

Greg had actually tried to find the answer to this question before he and Emily flew to Massachusetts. "I am told that if arrested, she will get nothing less than 25 years in federal prison. In prison, she might be safe from the Russians, who would like her dead, period. But that would ruin their family life."

"Did you ever meet Angelina in San Diego?"

"No, and she doesn't appear anything like the photo we saw of her." Greg noticed a flash of a smile crossed Baiev's face and quickly disappeared. "How is Colton doing? Does he seem happy?"

"Yes," Baiev chuckled, "He's completely happy. He loves being a father."

"He has always been so dedicated to his work. Emily and I have trouble thinking of him not working for two years."

"Oh, he has been working."

"What?"

"Yes, he's helping me create a Chechen-Russian dictionary."

"Good heavens!"

Before Greg and Emily left, Colton showed them both the dictionary he and Baiev were working on. One of the upstairs bedrooms had been converted into a workroom with two long desks: papers and books piled everywhere.

"Oh, yes," Emily said, "this room looks like Colton's."

* * *

Greg must have snoozed, because Emily had nudged him. The flight attendant was asking him if he wanted a drink. Awake again, he asked Emily if she got the story of how Colton and Angelina got married.

"Yes…let's see…Baiev and Yeza asked their imam to come to the house to marry them. The iman made sure they were registered at Needham's Town Hall."

* * *

Two years later, Colton and Angelina were living in Berkeley, California. Colton was working under a professor in the Slavic Languages Department of the University of California. He was being paid to complete, with Baiev's long-distance assistance, an English-Chechen dictionary. The internet, Skype, and email helped them coordinate their work.

Angelina was a stay-at-home mom who spent much of her spare time with the Native Plant Society in Berkeley. Regretfully, she couldn't return to Quietwater. Angelina said she would give anything (except her life) to walk Laika around the lakes again.

Greg and Emily, as well as the Khassens, visited the young family frequently. The children were blessed to have two sets of grandparents.

On her next camping trip with Phil and Linda, Thelma decided enough time had elapsed for her to get Phil to admit that Colton had 'turned' Lena to cooperating with the FBI. (Thelma had kept on investigating 'the case,' on her own time, of course.) Phil, damn him, only opened his mouth to hotdogs, potato chips, or s'mores.

The End

Epilogue

For many years, Frank Offenbacher wished he hadn't had the Hansens as neighbors. He had been afraid of Steve. After the Hansen house was abandoned and George's car was taken away, the Hansen home started to trouble Frank in another way. The shades had been pulled down over every window and no one ever went in or out. It bothered him even more when Susannah died in 2007. After that, he and Felice were all alone.

Frank noticed Felice made nightly trips into the Hansen yard. He once found her up on the Hansen's deck begging to be let in the sliding door. He knew no one was in the house. Can a cat's memory or feelings of attachment last that long, he wondered?

About the Book

For me writing a book is somewhat like making sourdough bread. I start with a human rights issue or an historical event about which little is known. It ferments in my mind while a story develops. Slowly, I knead it. The story expands large enough to be written down.

With *Intersecting Parallels,* the starting culture was the Chechen wars. Russia claimed it was combating internal Islamic terrorists, but the investigative journalist, Anna Politkovskaya, discovered other explanations and reported evildoing on both the Russian and the Chechen sides. She was jailed, tortured, and slipped a Mickey Finn to prevent her helping to broker a peace. Bullets from an assassin silenced her permanently in 2006. The character Katya Drozdov was modeled after Anna.

Dr. Baeiv Khassen is a real person. Like Anna, he didn't take sides but operated on any wounded person who came his way during the Chechen wars, holding true to the Hippocratic Oath. My description of his life once he moved to the United States is fictitious. To set the story in Russia was impractical, so I chose a place closer to home, in fact home—the HOA where I live in San Diego.

Acknowledgements

There are several people who helped me with *Intersecting Parallels* along the way. I especially thank Charles and Susannah Jeffery. They, along with Chris Ball, educated me about law enforcement details. I also appreciate the input of Francesca Turco, Joanna Brown, and Kevin Kirch. Last and far from least, I am most grateful for the editing skills and support of my publisher, Plowshare Media in La Jolla, California.

About the Author

Pamelia Barratt grew up in Chicago and spent summers on her father's cranberry bog in northern Wisconsin. After graduating from Smith College and receiving an advanced degree from Georgetown University, she taught chemistry in Washington, D.C. Later, while living in England, she earned a masters degree in Latin American Studies and, with her husband, established an NGO in Bolivia that helps indigenous Aymara people. Retirement has finally given her the opportunity to write mystery novels. *Intersecting Parallels* marks her sixth.

For additional information, please visit her website at:
http://pameliabarratt.com/

www.ingramcontent.com/pod-product-compliance
Lightning Source LLC
Chambersburg PA
CBHW070513260626
47161CB00004B/1532